"Don't play games with me, Sarah!"

It was the first time he'd ever called her by her given name, and it made her stomach do a curious flip. "Would it be too much to ask why you've granted me this visit?" Sarah asked nervously, acutely aware of his nearness.

"To give you some free advice," Guy said finally. "Be careful about what you write, Sarah. You can do a great deal of damage through ignorance. Stick to chatty little descriptions of lifeboat drills."

"You know," she said softly, "you really are insufferable. How dare you dictate what I can and cannot write!"

His voice was deep and disturbing. "Don't try to deceive me, Sarah. You know what I'm talking about."

But she *didn't* know then all that he was hiding....

LINDA HARREL
is also the author of this
Harlequin Romance

2337—SEA LIGHTNING

Arctic Enemy

by

LINDA HARREL

Harlequin Books

TORONTO • LONDON • LOS ANGELES • AMSTERDAM
SYDNEY • HAMBURG • PARIS • STOCKHOLM • ATHENS • TOKYO

Original hardcover edition published in 1981
by Mills & Boon Limited

ISBN 0-373-02459-2

Harlequin edition published February 1982

CHAPTER ONE

SARAH GREY placed a neat sheaf of papers on the secretary's desk. 'Done,' she said, 'and I've never been so delighted to have an assignment behind me.'

The young girl smiled and shook a halo of blonde curls. 'Complaints, Sarah? Not from you, surely!'

Sarah knew her boss's secretary held a resolutely romantic view of the life of a science reporter. 'Trish,' she said firmly, 'a study of recycling our mountains of waste is hardly a glamorous assignment. Not that I'm against it, mind you, but days spent in rubber boots prowling catwalks while miles of garbage-laden conveyor belts rumble on beneath you is not my idea of fun. Nor, I might add, is it likely to win me national acclaim as a scintillating writer.'

Trish, unmoved, grinned and flicked an impatient wrist. 'No matter,' she said breezily, 'your next story should more than make up for your days on the trash circuit.'

Sarah straightened her back, alert as a doe. 'D'Arcy's got something for me?'

'Yes—but I can't say another word. He practically made me take a vow of silence on this one.

So do me a favour, will you, and go in there and
speak to him? I'll see that your story gets filed.'

Sarah slid off the corner of Trish's desk, re-
vealing a trim curve of calf beneath the tailored
wool skirt—a fact not unnoticed by Terry West,
filing a story on pre-season hockey training in
Montreal, nor half a dozen other males busy that
morning in the *Herald*'s editorial offices. But
Sarah, as usual, had her mind on work and was
blind to the wistful glances. She knocked, waited
for the usual barked reply, and went into her
employer's office, instantly shutting out the clan-
gour of telephones and typewriters, and shouts
for copy boys.

The *Herald*'s managing editor looked up from
under an untidy shock of salt and pepper hair,
smiled ever so briefly, and indicated with a stab
of his finger the chair across from him.

As she settled into the leather chair, she said
easily, 'Trish has been tantalising me with hints
of a new assignment, D'Arcy. Is this more of her
irrepressible romanticism, or have you got a real
plum?'

He hesitated just a second. 'It's possible,' he
conceded gruffly. 'Does the name Tony Freeland
ring a bell?'

Sarah frowned, then brightened. 'In shipping,
isn't he? . . . Wait a second . . . of course! He was
the one who represented Freeland Shipping at
that big news conference last year on the Arctic
gas project, wasn't he?'

'He was,' D'Arcy agreed. 'Stood in for his uncle, Julian Freeland, the chairman of the board, who was ill. Well, he was back in Ottawa last week while you were off poking around in people's trash pails.'

'About the gas project again?'

'Yes—last-minute details with some government types about the maiden voyage of Freeland's ice-breaking super-tanker. And, being the aggressive newsman that I am, I cornered him over at the Parliament Building to feel him out about press coverage of their first trip into the Arctic.'

The implications of D'Arcy's news were not lost on Sarah, who leaned towards him intently. 'Oh, D'Arcy, you didn't get him to agree, did you? What a scoop—this has got to be one of the biggest stories in the world right now!'

Her boss allowed himself a rare smile. 'I did, as a matter of fact. And between you and me, I'm still somewhat stunned myself. This voyage, as you well know, is the most controversial in seafaring history. I expected Freeland to be leery, if not downright hostile, to the idea of close press coverage.'

'Close . . . just how close, D'Arcy?' Sarah's voice was very quiet.

D'Arcy Turner picked up his pipe and studied it. 'What would you say, Sarah, to accompanying the *Arctic Enterprise* on her maiden voyage. With an exclusive on the entire story?'

For once, Sarah Grey was speechless. She sank

back into the chair, the wide lavender eyes enormous.

Her boss chuckled and picked up the slack. 'I know,' he said nodding. 'The most I'd hoped for was some pre-sailing interviews, a tour of the ship. And I'd planned to fly a reporter and photographer up to the Arctic to cover the docking and loading operations, of course. But Freeland is actually willing to have a reporter on board.'

Sarah turned her head to one side on the delicate, ivory neck and looked askance at D'Arcy. 'And you're really giving the job to me?' she asked breathlessly.

At this, the amiable manner vanished and the gruff, irascible one for which D'Arcy Turner was both famed and feared returned. 'I'll tell you straight out, Sarah, that I'm not entirely happy with the thought of sending you out on this assignment, for lots of reasons.'

'Is there someone else you'd prefer?' she asked, unsuccessfully trying to conceal her alarm.

D'Arcy knocked his pipe against the rim of the large, pottery ashtray. 'There's Ted Benson, of course, who's qualified. He's out in Calgary doing a piece on nuclear energy, but I could recall him.' Anticipating her protest, he added quickly, 'But you are the one who's been covering the exploration for natural gas—you've got all the data at your fingertips. And there's another point in your favour—young Freeland himself.'

Sarah raised a perplexed eyebrow. 'Tony? In what way?'

'He remembered you from that press conference. I got the distinct impression that knowing you would land the job was a spur to giving his consent. He didn't say it in so many words, of course, but the implication was there.'

'There were dozens of us there that day. I don't see how he could remember me out of that sea of raised hands.'

D'Arcy smiled. 'You aimed some very good questions at the gentleman that day, my dear. Apparently he's not forgotten the reporter who did her homework.'

'He acquitted himself rather well, as I recall,' retorted Sarah. 'Perhaps a bit too smoothly, even. But my being a woman—that won't throw a monkey wrench into more practical shipboard matters?'

'No, he was quite definite about that. In fact, he said there'll be two other women, officers' wives, on board. But Sarah. I still don't know, on purely personal grounds, if I want you on that great monster of a super-tanker with its belly full of liquid gas up there in a sea mined with icebergs. It sounds bloody suicidal.'

Sarah set the firm little chin at a defiant angle. 'I thought the whole thrust of the engineers' arguments last year when this project was so hotly debated was the safety of the tanker. Because of the horrendous consequences of a gas explosion,

this is supposed to be the most carefully orches-
trated shipping adventure ever undertaken!'

'I know, I know.' He shrugged his shoulders.

Sarah crossed her legs and turned her eyes on
her boss. 'You didn't show such touching concern
for my safety last month when I flew to British
Columbia on that logging industry story—there
was a million times more chance of my plane
crashing than there's supposed to be of this super-
tanker exploding. And besides,' she pressed, 'if
it's safety you're really worried about, may I
remind you that Ted Benson is the father of three
young children while I'm alone in the world,
independent and very unmarried. Besides, I'll not
get anywhere in this business shrinking from the
thought of what *might* happen. You're a dear to
worry about me, D'Arcy, but please—I want this.
Very much.'

Shrugging again, D'Arcy pulled open his top
drawer.

'Time's a bit of a problem, so I've had Trish
make the preliminary arrangements. She's been
in touch with Freeland Shipping's executive
offices in London. Here's your itinerary, plane
ticket, plus a list of clothing they suggest. Trish
also has an expenses cheque waiting for you.' He
handed a plump manilla folder to her.

'Freeland finished construction of the *Arctic
Enterprise* last month in their Japanese shipyards.
They've just finished bringing her on sea trials
from there to Rotterdam for some last-minute

utfitting and taking on supplies. You're to fly to
Rotterdam and board her there two days from
now.'

Sarah scanned the itinerary, shaking the glossy
curtain of hair. 'Through the English Channel,
north past Greenland to Baffin Bay, and on to
Melville Island. The old Northwest Passage that
very Canadian school child knows by heart!
It makes you shiver, doesn't it, D'Arcy, just to
think about those old sailing ships trying to find
passage through the Arctic to the Orient?
It's everybody's dream to really see it some
day.'

'Well, not everyone's, perhaps. It's not exactly a
tropical cruise. But it does have a certain adventuresome ring to it, I'll grant you.'

Sarah shot him a knowing look. 'You don't fool
me for a minute. If you weren't saddled with
managing this paper you'd have grabbed your
pencil and parka and been off on this one yourself!
Which reminds me: two days is nothing at all.
I've got research to do, files to pull—not to men-
tion all this shopping and packing!'

And so she thanked him, promised him the best
exclusive he'd ever seen, blew him a kiss, and
vanished into the windowless depths of the newspaper file room.

There, she snapped the plastic lid off her coffee
container and took a small sip. In her quick, neat
fashion she sorted the folders and stacks of micro-
film the library clerk had piled on to the long

wooden table, rejecting some, setting others aside.

With her chin resting on her tiny hand, she re-read the story she herself had written the year before on the tapping of the Arctic's trillions of cubic feet of natural gas. The engineers she had interviewed were just completing work on a mammoth refrigeration plant on Melville Island that would liquify the gas at a temperature of minus a hundred and sixty degrees Celsius and pump it into waiting tankers.

At first, they had thought that the process could only take place during the brief period when the northern waters were relatively ice-free. But then they had devised the ambitious plan to build giant ice-breaking super-tankers that would turn a limited venture into a profitable year-round one.

Bitter controversy had swirled around the project from the beginning. Promoters claimed it heralded a new era of technology for the world while offering Canada security and independence at a time of frightening energy scarcity.

But detractors questioned the impact the project would have on the fragile ecology of the Arctic. Darkly, some even hinted that it was only a matter of time before there would be a cata-strophic explosion of the liquid natural gas, or L.N.G. They likened it to a nuclear holocaust which would create unspeakable horror, wiping out wildlife and threatening the entire chain of life. And then there was the native peoples' con-

cern for their rights and way of life, a sensitive
and complex issue, to be sure.

After acrimonious debate, the project had won
approval, although the conditions for it were to
be stringent. The liquification plant was to be
remote from human settlement. The route of the
super-tanker would avoid as far as possible both
the human population and the rich herds of
whales, seals and caribou.

But in nothing would the safeguards be as ex-
tensive as they would be for the construction of
the L.N.G. tankers. That, at least, was reassuring,
thought Sarah, slipping the article back into its
folder and pulling the file on Freeland Shipping
towards her.

The fact that Freeland Shipping had won the
contract to produce and run the world's first ice-
breaking super-tanker had been a surprise to
everyone involved. The staggering construction
and operating costs of super-tankers, running into
millions of dollars, meant that they were almost
always backed by giant financial consortiums. But
Freeland was the exception—one of the last great
family-owned shipping enterprises. Their ships
were all of British registry, also a rarity at a time
when more and more owners had 'flags of convenience' from countries where standards weren't
as high as they remained in Britain. Freeland
Shipping still stood for all that was best in the
traditions of the sea. Its liners remained the
grande dames of the ocean, embodying the

romantic mystique that others had abandoned long ago in favour of speed and efficiency.

But Freeland had been eclipsed during the previous ten years by the aggressive newcomers, the multi-billion dollar conglomerates that dominated the heady world of super-tankers. No one in that closed circle had thought that Freeland would reach the final round of fierce bidding for the contract.

But make it they did, with a superb presentation on the most expensive ship ever to be built. It was to be a Class 7 ice-breaker, one able to navigate waters encrusted with ice up to seven feet in depth. No ship in the world was to have more sophisticated navigation or safety equipment gracing its decks.

The superiority of design and the best estimated date of completion, combined with Freeland's reputation for impeccable standards, had won them the contract hands down. There was a rash of raised eyebrows and tempers in the exclusive club of super-tanker owners.

'Impressive,' murmured Sarah, flipping through the pages of an obscure shipping industry quarterly. And even more impressive was the role played in the company's resurgence by Tony Freeland himself. Although his uncle was the major stockholder and dominant figure in the company, Julian Freeland's increasingly poor health had forced him to relinquish more and more control to his nephew. It was Tony, appar-

ently, who was singlehandedly responsible for
Freeland's furious fight for the L.N.G. contract
and its bid to win back a leading role in world
shipping.

Sarah's delicate fingers, the nails free of polish
and buffed to a pearly glow, pulled a photographer's glossy proof out of the *Herald*'s picture
file. A group of government officials together with
representatives of Freelands smiled out at her.
They were gathered in an ornately panelled office
for the contract signing ceremony.

Sarah was suddenly and intensely curious about
the man who had approved her presence aboard
the *Enterprise* at such a critical time, and who was
to be her host for the voyage. She bent over the
picture, her arched eyebrows coming together in
a tiny frown of concentration, and tried to pick
out the frustratingly small details. With her reporter's training, she scanned the faces, searching
for expression, gestures, anything that might give
her an insight into what was really going on
behind the amiable public façade.

Seated in the centre of the group was an elderly,
distinguished gentleman who the caption confirmed was Julian. Beside him, documents in hand
and obviously in charge, sat the urbane and darkly
handsome man she recognised as Tony. The rest
were identified only as other government and
company representatives.

They all, with one glaring exception, looked
jubilant. The exception stood towards the rear of

the assemblage, his bearing stiff and his otherwise attractive face askew with a slight grimace. An unfortunate camera angle, Sarah concluded, for surely everyone at that signing must have been dizzy with elation.

She turned her attention back to Tony Freeland and discovered that the prospect of being his guest for a few weeks was not entirely unpleasant. He had handled himself beautifully at their encounter the year before, smoothly fielding difficult and frequently hostile questions from the press.

She had wondered at the time if his manner wasn't too unruffled to be genuine. But then, she reasoned, he had ample cause for that supreme confidence. If the rumours were true that his company had been on the verge of bankruptcy and he alone had saved it with this staggeringly ambitious venture, who could fault him for crowing a bit? He had to be a remarkable man. With any luck at all, she was going to have a blockbuster story on her hands.

CHAPTER TWO

THE *Arctic Enterprise* had grown and grown, as the taxi picked its way down the littered dock at dawn, until she seemed to fill the horizon. She blotted out the pale slice of sun rising over Rotterdam's Europort and even seemed to muffle the squalling, reeling gulls.

Empty of cargo and riding high, her steel walls formed a cold, grey canyon. Sarah stood at the bottom of that canyon, her neck tipped painfully back as she strained to catch a glimpse of the living and navigational superstructure that loomed like a modern office tower high over the stern.

'Designed for beauty you weren't,' she murmured, noting critically the graceless and utilitarian lines. Only the fine gold lettering of the Freeland crest emblazoned on the rakish funnel and the regal crimson of the house flag snapping smartly in the breeze were reminders of the flair and elegance that marked Freeland's passenger liners. Had it pained that traditionalist, Julian Freeland, to put his seal on so exotic yet oddly plain a ship? Sarah wondered.

The driver deposited the last of her luggage at her feet and slammed the car trunk shut. Sarah puzzlèd a moment over the strange currency, then produced the fare from her change purse. '*Bedankt,*' she said, smiling.

The man touched his hand to the peak of his cap and then drove off, tossing a last, perplexed glance over his shoulder. Stylish young foreigners were not his usual passengers to this part of town.

One thing that had not changed on Freeland ships, Sarah observed, was discipline. Around her buzzed intense preparations for departure. A drove of uniformed men scurried about obeying the shouted orders. But it was a controlled chaos, cheerful and expectant, that contrasted sharply with the confused and ill-tempered activity across the pier where another outward bound tanker was preparing to sail.

'Miss Grey?' A smartly uniformed officer with a crewman in tow had appeared out of nowhere. 'I was told to keep a very sharp eye out for you. Your flight was pleasant, I hope?'

'Yes—very, thank you, although a bit rushed.'

The young man grinned shyly. 'You'll have lots of time to unwind once we're under way. That's the beauty of ships.' He motioned to the cadet, who moved briskly to heft her luggage. 'If you'll come with me, please, I have instructions to take you directly to Mr Freeland's suite.'

Sarah took one last look skyward at the *Enterprise* before leaving the ground she would not touch again for many days.

'A bit daunting the first time, isn't it?' the officer acknowledged, noting her hesitation at the gangplank.

'A little,' she conceded. 'I memorised all the statistics—the length and tonnage and so on. But it didn't prepare me for the impact of its size at all! I suppose you've become very blasé about it by now.'

'No,' he replied bluntly. 'I don't think we ever get used to these monsters.' The smile touched his lips but not his eyes.

Suddenly Sarah recalled an expression from a book she had read, that ships sometimes use when they see another headed for trouble. 'You are standing into danger,' they flash. What a thing to have pop into her mind! she thought. She shrugged it off, raised her tiny chin, and began the long climb into the bowels of the *Arctic Enterprise*.

Great, seemingly endless lengths of gleaming corridor shot off into the distance. Down one of them, her luggage had vanished. She would never orientate herself, she fretted. The windowless maze gave no hint of level or direction. What she needed, she concluded, was one of those 'You Are Here' signs they post in huge buildings. Or per-haps a trail of breadcrumbs.

Around one corner was the surprise of a sleek rosewood and smoked glass elevator that shot them silently into the giddy height of the stern living tower. She had been half skipping to keep pace with the energetic gait of the officer, and

now she braked herself to keep from crashing into
him. He had stopped at a door that was the
stunning exception to the row upon row of
anonymous beige metal ones they had passed.

This was a broad, double door, carved from
polished teak and rich with heavy brass fittings.
The officer rapped smartly.

'Come!'

He entered, stood back respectfully, and presented her with a remarkable scene. In contrast to
the artificial glow of the halls, this room was
awash with the dazzling pink light of the sunrise,
admitted by a wall of broad windows. Before the
windows was a grouping of opulent modern sofas
and chairs of tobacco brown leather. Under foot
was thick cream broadloom. The panelled walls
were hung with ornately framed oils of sailing
ships. At the far side of the room, a doorway
revealed a glimpse of hallway and bedrooms
opening off of it. In this arch stood the man who
had brought her here, Anthony Freeland.

His smile was immediate and disarming.
'You've made it, Miss Grey! How delightful to see
you again after—what is it—almost two years
now? Welcome aboard the *Arctic Enterprise*!'

He came towards her, a slim, well-manicured
hand outstretched.

'Thank you, Mr Freeland. I'm very pleased,
and grateful, to be here.'

'It's Tony—please,' he said. 'We're going to be
travelling companions for some time. And may I

call you Sarah?'

She smiled her assent and took the seat he indicated on the sofa nearest the windows. As he dis-
missed her escort, she took him in with a sweep
of her professional eye. He was the first man
she'd seen in civilian dress, a superbly tailored
dark suit that fitted the tall, thin body to perfection. His finely chiselled features were framed by
longish black hair swept back from greying
temples.

Nothing out of place, she noted. A man to
whom control was very important. The patrician
accent, the refinement, gave him an aura of tremendous power and success. Physically, at least,
Tony Freeland seemed equal to the legend that
had sprung up about him recently.

The greying hair, the purposefulness and confidence of his manner were usually marks of the
older man. But up close, Sarah could see that he
was probably no more than thirty-five or six. That
much was a shock.

He settled beside her, one leg crossed casually
over the other, and locked his eyes on her. She
realised with a start that he was genuinely pleased
to see her. Oddly, that knowledge unsettled rather
than reassured her. She was so accustomed to the
objects of her interviews treating her with suspicion, or at least a touch of nervousness. Tony
Freeland was very sure of himself.

They exchanged polite small talk and accepted
coffee from a white-jacketed steward who served

them and vanished as silently as he had appeared. It was a seductively relaxed and luxurious atmosphere that invited lingering. But Sarah was growing increasingly restive. Outside that hushed suite, she knew the ship was vibrating with the preparations for departure, and she wanted to be a witness to all of it.

Setting her gold-rimmed cup down beside the sterling coffee service, she tactfully shifted the tone of their conversation.

'This is delightful, Tony, but I'm afraid this is a working day for me—D'Arcy indicated that my capacity here is to be that of an independent reporter, covering the voyage as I see fit. Would it be fair to say that this is your understanding as well?'

'Absolutely,' he agreed. 'You are responsible only to your newspaper. With one caution.'

Sarah shifted uneasily. Here we go, she thought—strings. 'And that is?' she asked pleasantly.

'I've arranged for you to have liberal access to all areas of the *Enterprise*. But you'll be subject to the rules that bind all of us on board. The operation of this ship is a very complicated business. There may be times when your presence might be . . . well, distracting, shall we say. So in matters of the ship's operations, you'll have to follow the instructions of the officers to the letter.'

His words were discreet, but the gaze that slid the length of her conveyed his meaning precisely.

Sarah was faintly irritated, but relieved as well that the controls over her would be of a practical, not editorial, nature.

'I assure you, Tony, that I have no intention of becoming a liability on this voyage.'

'I don't doubt that at all,' he replied easily. 'And while there'll be the usual lifeboat drills and such as the law demands, I'm sure they'll be nothing more than a formality.'

Sarah saw her opening and took it. 'Then you dismiss the critics who claim the *Enterprise* could cause an astronomical disaster?' She slipped her hand into her leather portfolio and produced a pen and notepad. She looked at him and saw him nod almost imperceptibly. Wordlessly, they had made the transition from casual conversation to professional interview.

'Doomsayers, the lot,' he replied crisply. He offered her a cigarette, was refused, and lit his own with a slim, gold lighter. The gesture exposed a fine, tanned wrist covered with thick black hair, striking against the starched white shirt cuff.

'And I'll say more,' he continued, leaning back lazily. 'They're a bunch of ill-informed spoilers who, if they had their way, would send the entire world straight back to the Dark Ages. I mean that quite literally! You can't put a stranglehold on technology. Unless we keep after these new sources of energy, we're going to run out—and soon! That won't mean a romantic return to

nature. It will mean hunger and suffering on a
scale never known before.'

'But there *are* dangers,' she pressed. 'And no
one has ever attempted what you're going to do
on this voyage. You must be facing many unknowns.'

If the persistence bothered him, he was hiding
it very well, she thought. But despite the un-
hesitating smile, she was sure there was something
disturbingly tight and unyielding about his jaw-
line.

'Of course,' he conceded, but an impatient gesture of his hand showed what he thought of them.
'There've been unknowns and risks in every
worthwhile venture ever undertaken by man.
What it comes down to is that there's a time,
Sarah, when the balance shifts in favour of taking
those risks. The world is at that point now!'

'You have quite a personal stake in this,' Sarah
noted, observing the intensity that unexpectedly
sparked his voice.

'I do,' he confirmed with a sudden laugh.
'Overseeing the construction of the *Enterprise*,
against considerable odds, has been the consum-
ing interest of my life for the last few years.'

Sarah brushed back a strand of auburn hair that
had fallen across her brow as she bent over her
pad. She looked at him appraisingly. 'The obstacles,' she said quickly, picking up the lead he
had wittingly, or unwittingly offered to her.
'Besides the fierce competition you had from

other shipping lines, was there any opposition within Freeland itself? Your uncle, for example. How did he feel about this rather dramatic departure from Freeland tradition?'

A faint veil of irritation might have fallen over his pale eyes, but Sarah could not be sure. Certainly the measured, cultured speech did not alter.

'My uncle, as you may know, has not been as well as we would like during the last few years. While he didn't take an active part in the development of the *Enterprise*, he didn't oppose it. He was, in fact, an invaluable adviser. Uncle Julian stands for all that's best in maritime tradition. I like to think that in the *Enterprise*, we've successfully merged his standards from the past with the most brilliant technology available today.'

'What you're really saying, then, is that this ship is essentially your doing.'

He looked down, grinding out the cigarette. Modesty? Evasiveness? 'No one man can claim full credit for a project as vast as this,' he said at last. 'But your assumption is basically correct. Given Freeland's reputation and record, I felt it was virtually our moral responsibility to assume this contract.'

'Despite the fact that you've been overshadowed recently by larger shipping concerns?' Yes, she thought, there it was again, that slight clouding of the eyes, a thinning of the lips. The

question had definitely nettled. She continued to
hold his gaze, silently demanding a response. It was
not, she had learned from painful experience, her job
to win popularity contests.

'You may be confusing quality with a rather
reckless display of naval showmanship, Sarah.
Freeland Shipping has *never* been bettered. These
newcomers with their dubious credentials and
anonymous financial backers have no business in
a matter which bears directly on world peace and
stability. Your own góvernment understood that
very well when it chose us.'

Once again the confident smile. Diplomatically,
Sarah returned it. But in truth she was less than
satisfied with the smooth reply that neatly side-
stepped the real thrust of her question by focus-
sing instead on the alleged weaknesses of his competition. Could he really be that sure of himself,
so immune to the barrage of criticism that had
been levelled at him?

Quickly Sarah weighed her options and decided
on silence. She would not challenge him further.
At least, not yet. Nor would she expose just how
thoroughly she had researched the L.N.G. project. That would risk making him pull up his
guard with her, perhaps killing from the outset
her chance of getting a story from him with some
real meat to it.

'Now,' he said, rising and offering his hand to
her, 'why don't I take you up to the bridge to
meet our master and senior officers? We'll be

getting under way shortly, and I'm sure you'll want to record that—it's a very exciting experience. Afterwards we'll give you the grand tour.' He glanced at her tiny feet, neated shod in fine dress pumps. 'You may want to change into more casual clothes once we're out to sea. It does get rough sometimes, and your balance may be a little shaky in those, charming as they are.'

'Yes, I intend to,' she replied, 'just as soon as I'm reunited with my luggage.'

'It's not far from here, actually. I've put you in one of the unused senior officers' cabins on the deck just below this. Oh . . . I should add you'll be taking meals in the officers' wardroom. We do dress for that. Not formally, precisely, but the men wear full uniform for the evening 'pour out', as we call it. And the women usually change from pants into dresses. Just another Freeland custom we like to keep alive.'

'Sounds lovely,' said Sarah, favouring him with a smile.

'It is, rather. And if you happen to have any questions about personal matters, you could ask either Mrs Price or Mrs McQuade. I expect you'll be meeting them shortly.'

Remarkable! she thought, as she followed after him. Bound for the Arctic on a floating gas tank; and we dress for the cocktail hour! Perhaps this wasn't destined to be a dry tale of numbers and scientific jargon after all. Once again she marvelled at the luck that had brought her here. Any

lingering misgiving that she might have har-
boured evaporated.

Formal dinners, liveried stewards, and a host
who was gracious, undeniably handsome, and
cheerfully handing her the story of a lifetime on a
silver platter. Her colleagues back in the news-
room had teased her with visions of a frostbitten
nose and notes painfully scribbled by mittened
hands on a cold, creaking barge of a boat. If they
only knew!

It was an odd mixture—a little like the ships'
bridges shown in old war movies, a little like a
space-age laboratory. The ship's wheel of an earlier era had vanished, replaced by a small, discreet
lever. A massive stainless steel bank of equipment
stretched the entire width of the bridge, pulsing
with a bewildering array of blinking lights and
glowing dials. An officer sat before a computer
console, punching data into it as responses flashed
instantly across its screen. Sarah picked out the
long and short range radar, the Loran navigation
equipment, the collision avoidance system, the
gyro-compass. The rest she couldn't begin to
fathom.

The Captain's chair was much as she had
imagined it would be, large and imposing, raised
above the rest of the room on a small platform. It
faced a wall of outward slanting windows which
overlooked the main deck far below.

The man in it sat erect, his immaculate Navy
uniform heavily ornamented with gold braid. In a

quiet yet commanding voice, he conducted the activities of a dozen lesser officers and cadets.

A very young man wearing, astonishingly, the mark of a senior officer, stood alertly at the Master's elbow, clipboard and pencil raised. The sharp blue eyes under a shock of carroty hair caught the arrival of the two civilians instantly. Inclining slightly towards his superior he said, 'Captain Price, sir. Mr Freeland is here . . . with his guest.'

There was an instant silence on the bridge as every eye turned their way. Slowly, the Master swivelled in the great, padded chair, causing a quick return to industriousness by his crew.

He was a small, precise man, with military carriage and intense, intelligent eyes. Sarah speculated that his calm, quiet manner was backed by an anger that could be fearful when aroused.

'Captain Price,' said Tony, 'may I present Sarah Grey, the reporter from the Ottawa paper. Sarah, this is our Master, Captain John Price, the finest commander on the seas today.'

The Master cast a somewhat jaundiced eye at Tony, but smiled. And while he accepted Sarah's hand graciously, he did not rise.

'You have explained to Miss Grey about the rules governing passengers, Mr Freeland?' he asked.

'In general,' Tony confirmed, and Sarah quickly added,

'I'll be as inconspicuous as possible, Captain

Price. I would hate to have my presence in-
convenience anyone.'

'Nonsense,' interjected Tony. 'I'm sure
Captain Price shares our pleasure at having the
Enterprise given all the attention she deserves.'
Tony's chin lifted as he spoke, his pride and en-
thusiasm evident.

Like many people who shoulder great responsibility, John Price was a man of few words.
'She's a fine ship,' he said simply. Then, 'The
tide is with us now, Mr Freeland. I expect the
Rotterdam harbour pilot at any moment. If you'll
excuse me . . .'

He turned his back to them, the meeting
abruptly terminated, and was once again totally
immersed in the workings of the bridge. Tony and
Sarah retreated to a corner as the pace quickened.

That brief journey in or out of port is the time
of greatest danger for a ship. No captain could
possibly know all the hidden shoals and treacherous currents of every harbour into which he sails.
The prickly job of steering a course through the
maze of harbour traffic falls to the pilot.

Captain Price stood to one side, having yielded
his chair, with elaborate courtesy, to the
Enterprise's temporary commander. Tony leaned
against a table, his arms crossed carelessly across
his chest, but Sarah caught the rhythmic pulsing
of the muscle in his jaw and knew he was anything
but relaxed. The young First Officer, Patrick
McQuade, watched the ship's clock as if the next

sweep of the second hand would detonate a bomb. Tension flowed in waves from all of them. Sarah felt herself infected by it. The anticipation was excruciating, yet somehow delicious as well.

'O-eight-double-o!' Patrick shouted, startling her. He made a note in a large book. 'Log begun, sir,' he said.

The pilot's voice rang out. 'Wheel fifteen degrees to port.' His command was followed by a double echo from the First Officer and the helmsman.

'Let go the lines!'

The order was relayed by crackling radio, and six floors below and a quarter of a mile ahead, the ant-like figures of the crew could be seen scrabbling across the bows, handling the fat lines with a frenzy that contrasted dramatically with the ritual calm of the bridge. Muffled shouts rose up from the stern.

'Slow ahead,' intoned the pilot.

'Slow ahead,' his chorus responded.

Five sea-going tugs nuzzled the *Enterprise* like tiny animals against a mother. Reluctantly, the great bulk swung out in a wide arc, stern first, from the pier.

'Half ahead.'

Slowly, slowly, the *Enterprise* moved forward.

Their job accomplished, the tugs fell back. In unison, they sounded a raucous salute. Hearing the *Enterprise*'s resonant reply, they foamed the water beneath them and churned back to shore.

Having safely disengaged his charge from the dock, the pilot ordered a course. 'Full speed ahead,' he ended.

'Aye, aye.'

The bubble of tension that had enclosed all of them broke. There would be no beaching of the ship on a hidden sandbar, no scraping of the fresh, unblemished paint. The burden of authority shifted once more.

'Nicely done, Mr Danner!' said Captain Price, pouring coffee for both of them.

'She's a responsive vessel, Captain. I hadn't thought she would be.'

'She was designed by the greatest naval architect in the world,' said Tony, coming forward to join them. 'I for one am not surprised that she handles beautifully.'

Mr Danner's shoulders lifted in an expressive shrug. 'Still, I don't know that I would like to be in your shoes,' he said, shaking his head. 'Moving through a well-charted port is one thing—but snaking your way through ice fields with a cargo like yours will be quite a challenge for you I think, Captain!'

'It will indeed,' conceded the Master cheerfully. The prospect didn't appear to daunt him in the slightest.

The harbour traffic thinned and the sea opened out before them. The captain ordered 'dead slow'. Gravely, he and the pilot shook hands, bringing down the curtain on their ticklish relationship.

While the ship's horn sounded a goodbye, the Jacob's ladder was lowered over the starboard side. Saluting jauntily, Mr Danner vanished over the side and into a waiting launch.

Their last link with land was gone. They were isolated now in their own floating community. With signal flags and house colours rippling from the bridge halyard, and the sky and sea as blue and beautiful as anyone could have wished, the bow was pointed towards the English Channel. Behind them, the coast was receding quickly into a thin, smoky line.

'We're on our way!' cried Patrick, charged with the sheer joy of setting off on an old-fashioned adventure.

Yes! thought Sarah, it's wonderful. She felt a little shiver of pleasure pass over her thin arms and hugged herself.

It was a single room, not the luxurious suite of the owner. But it conveyed the same sense of snug comfort. Sarah sank gratefully into the armchair and kicked off her shoes. 'Delicious!' she sighed, relishing the sudden hush and privacy after the bustle of the last few hours.

She glanced about her at the built-in bed, the crisp white sheets, the teak desk set thoughtfully beneath a porthole with a perfect view of the sea. Someone—she had yet to see who—had set her typewriter up on the desk, a pristine stack of paper and long, freshly sharpened pencils beside it. On

the coffee table sat a jug of ice water, two sparkl-
ing glasses, and a dish of plump purple grapes. A
reading light by her pillow glowed invitingly.

It was a perfect hideaway in which to order
her thoughts and set down her impressions while
they were still fresh. During her tour of the ship,
which took several hours to complete, she had
dutifully jotted down an avalanche of figures enthusiastically reeled off to her by Tony and the
crew.

But the *Enterprise*'s statistics, impressive
though they were, were not what intrigued her. It
was the spirit of the people who lived and worked
on her. To a man, from the highest officer to
engine room cadet, they had a pioneering sense of
dedication and pride. And she did not think that
it was just a dutiful response to being questioned
in front of the owner. No, Tony was someone who
awed them, she could tell. But they didn't seem
particularly bound to him personally.

She had been nothing short of staggered by the
fittings of the *Enterprise*. She had all the amenities
of a small city, with individual cabins for the crew,
game rooms, a library, movie theatre and hospital.

The officers had their own restricted section
that reminded Sarah of a smart private club. The
wardroom boasted a polished mahogany bar,
studded leather sofas, lush carpeting and curtains.

In the depths of the steel-banded hull, specially

reinforced to withstand the stresses of the icefields through which they would soon labour, Sarah saw engine-rooms and pump-rooms that looked more like space ship control centres than the sweaty boiler-rooms of the past.

The tour had ended on an odd note.

'I've worn you out,' Tony had said when they were finished and leaning lazily against the polished wood rail that swept around the flying bridge.

Sarah tilted her chin to the sun and shook her hair in the breeze. 'My feet, yes,' she admitted. 'But this air is exhilarating—so clear and brilliant! You're incredibly lucky, Tony, to have rooms waiting for you on each of your ships. If I were you, I'm afraid I'd spend all my time sailing to exotic places.'

Her head was just level with his shoulder. Tony smiled down at her and shrugged. 'I hate to dis-illusion you, but the novelty tends to pale after a while. I'm the sort who likes less confined com-forts, and a nice fast jet.'

'It's a waste,' Sarah pronounced. 'All those Freeland liners crisscrossing the globe with those huge—and empty—owner's suites.'

'I'd never thought of it like that,' he said. 'But you're right. I detest waste of any sort. So—they're yours. Any time you want.'

'Just like that?'

'Just like that. All you have to do is pick up a telephone and I'll arrange it ... Japan, India,

South Africa, any place in the world you want to
go.'

Sarah pulled her sweater over her head and shook
her red-brown hair back into place. Tony Freeland
had not laughed when he said that to her. He had
meant it. She stripped off the rest of her clothes and
considered what sort of a man he was.

So far he had given her virtually nothing to
complain about. He was open, helpful, almost
eager, really, to make her job easy. And he was
delightful company. Even her father, she thought
wryly, would find him thoroughly acceptable
company for his only daughter.

But this offer of a suite on his ships—surely
that was unnecessarily extravagant. Still, she
reasoned, Tony was probably accustomed to dic-
tating his own terms in everything he did. Grand
gestures could be made with careless ease by a
man like him.

She stepped into the shower and let the hot
water run in rivers down her tired body. One
thing seemed certain: she was not going to have
to dig and pry and cajole for every scrap of information. No one was going to be able to hint
that her story was just a whitewash of this part of
the L.N.G. project. Her respect for the
Enterprise's owner was beginning to grow.

She rubbed herself briskly with a thick towel,
urging life back into her still throbbing legs.
Fortunately, Freeland's home office had effici-

ently conveyed to Trish that the tradition of dressing for dinner was alive and well aboard their ships. Trish's typed clothing list had noted the need for what they called an 'afternoon dress' Typically, Trish had added, in her own hand, a string of enthusiastic and approving exclamation marks.

Sarah had packed two—enough was enough, she thought—and besides, she planned to take as many meals as possible alone in her cabin, pounding on her typewriter. Planned, that was, before she met Tony? a small voice inside her asked.

She gave a final tightening to the belt of the scarlet wool shirtwaister that flamed against the pale skin. Just right, she decided, twirling before the full-length mirror: soft and covered, but with a touch of dressiness in the colour and sling-back heels. She snapped tiny gold clips on her ears, grabbed her clutch bag, and headed for the officers' wardroom.

'I just love it. I mean, all the men looking so distinguished, and the talk of a storm that's brewing or a ship we passed on the last watch. And it means Patrick and I can have such a nice quiet time together—as if we were in our own living room!'

Her name was Katie McQuade. She looked not a day over nineteen and she was as pretty as a picture, with cornflower eyes under a froth of copper curls.

'This has always been my favourite time of the day too, Katie. Of course, I was a much older woman than you when I finally went to sea. John and I had raised our children by then.'

'I expect when Patrick and I start our family I'll have to give up these trips, too. In fact, this will probably be the only voyage I'll make on the *Enterprise*. Patrick says it may be rough once we get up to the Arctic Circle. Have you ever been across it, Emily?'

'Not once, my dear. This is an adventure I wouldn't miss for the world!'

Emily Price was a little brown wren of a woman, and just as friendly and charming. Her appealingly plump figure was almost swallowed up by the armchair in which she sat.

She turned and smiled at Sarah who sat next to her. 'John and I take most of our meals in our rooms, Sarah,' she said, 'but we always dine with the officers on the first night out.'

'And they appreciate it, Emily, they really do!' chirped Katie. 'It always seems so special—just like a party—when you and the Master eat with us. Patrick served under Captain Price on his last command, too,' she explained to Sarah, 'although that was on the Middle East run.'

'Captain Price sounds as if he's very much loved by his men,' Sarah observed, sipping her gin and tonic.

'Oh gosh, yes,' agreed Katie. 'I swear they'd walk the plank for him. Patrick always says if he develops into half the Master Captain Price is he'll be satisfied.'

Emily Price laughed delightedly, her pink cheeks dimpling. Sarah was utterly charmed by the *Enterprise*'s two other passengers. They were a generation apart, but they shared a common bond, a deep and obvious devotion to the two men who commanded the great ship.

Katie was touchingly young, glowing with the same idealism that illuminated the pleasant features of her husband. Emily possessed a natural wisdom and endearing warmth. Together, the women provided a circle of cheer and kindness that was relished in an otherwise hard and demanding man's world. Somehow, thought Sarah, she must find a way of weaving their feminine strand into the fabric of her story.

Just as the dinner chimes were trilling, the men appeared, brimming with high spirits. Captain Price himself extended his arm to Sarah and escorted her into the dining room.

'I've been hearing nothing but praise for you today, Captain,' she said.

'A loyal crew,' he quipped. 'I've trained them well!'

'You're too modest,' she teased. 'I didn't detect a hint of coercion. They seemed to speak from their hearts.'

The Master pulled back a chair for her. 'The hearts I leave entirely to my wife, Miss Grey,' he said, and Emily beamed shyly at him.

He took his place at the head of a long table set with a damask cloth and fine china. Tony sat at the foot with Katie and Sarah at either side. Shop talk was goodnaturedly banned, but the conversation returned to the voyage time and time again anyway. Toasts were raised repeatedly to its success.

Katie had joked to Sarah that Tony terrified her at their first meeting, with his urbane, almost haughty manners. But now, as he turned his considerable charm on to the women, and Katie's tinkling laughter rose above the hum of conversation, it was evident that she was captivated by him.

Sarah felt the spell, too. It was difficult not to believe they were caught up in a fairy-tale world. Even the food, from the fine consommé and grilled sole to the rich pastries for dessert, contributed to the feeling of privilege and fantasy.

Coffee was being poured and a silver platter of cheese and fruit passed when a cadet appeared and apologetically approached the Master.

'A radio communication from London, sir,' he said, standing stiffly at his side. 'It's from head office, for your attention only.'

Tony elevated a dark brow and shot a quizzical glance the length of the table. Conversation was politely muted as Captain Price accepted the sheet of paper, read, and nodded his dismissal of the messenger. His face was expressionless, betraying no hint of what he was thinking.

'Patrick,' he said, 'perhaps you would be good enough to read this aloud for the benefit of the officers . . . and Mr Freeland, of course. It will affect all of us in the days to come.'

Patrick took the paper, cleared his throat self-consciously, and read. '*To the Master*, Arctic Enterprise. *Prepare to accept the arrival by company helicopter, out of Southampton Harbour, of Captain Guy Court, for the purpose of carrying out safety inspection procedures. Please radio harbour authorities when you are passing within range. Signed, Julian Freeland.*'

Patrick pursed his lips as if to let out a long, silent whistle, then laid the paper neatly before him and looked quickly left and right. After a stunned silence, a reaction grew and rippled around the table. The men shook their heads and exchanged quiet, alarmed comments. Only the Master seemed unruffled and calmly sliced a wedge of cheese for his biscuit.

Tony's response, however, was immediate and a good deal less restrained. Crumpling his napkin roughly and scraping his chair back, he was visibly disbelieving and angry.

'This is damn poor judgement on someone's part, Captain!' he snapped, pulling the gold lighter out of his breast pocket with an irritable gesture. 'You and the men don't need any more problems right now—were you aware that this kind of non-sense was going to happen?'

'I was not, Mr Freeland,' the Master replied easily, sipping his coffee. 'It's as much a surprise to me as it is, I take it, to you.'

'My uncle said nothing to me,' Tony retorted, his lips thin with anger. 'Perhaps he himself didn't know until now. This sort of shabby tactics is more Guy's style than his.'

'You may have something there, although I don't think I would have characterised it in quite those terms.'

'Whatever,' said Tony dismissively. 'But since I estimate we must be just about below Southampton now, may I suggest that you do something quickly to put a stop to this?'

The Captain folded his hands before him and looked steadily at Tony. 'I'm sure I don't need to point out to you, Mr Freeland, that your uncle himself established the office of Safety Master as an independent authority within the company. Even if I wanted to, I couldn't prevent Captain Court's arrival.'

Tony shook his head vehemently. 'But it's insanity on a maiden voyage of this complexity!'

'Perhaps,' said Captain Price, shrugging, 'this is the very time when we should be welcoming Captain Court.'

Their Master's comments seemed to inspire debate among the officers, and whispered arguments broke out around the table.

Captain Price's tone became more conciliatory. 'I'll grant you,' he said, raising his hand for silence, 'that I hadn't been expecting Guy to appear until our second trip. But perhaps there's some method in his madness.'

He smiled, but it was not returned. The atmosphere in the room had altered irretrievably. The men sat silent and ill at ease. Emily tactfully busied herself with refilling coffee cups from the silver service in front of her. Katie was wide-eyed.

Sarah was fascinated by the dramatic change that had been wrought by one brief radio message. She stared at her companions with undisguised curiosity. Who was it who could so easily snarl the smoothly purring operation of the *Enterprise* and provoke such intense disagreement among its previously harmonious crew? The others obviously shared Tony's shock and disapproval.

She took a deep breath and plunged bravely into the awkward silence around her. 'Would I be out of line,' she began, 'if I asked just who this person is who's coming aboard?'

It was Patrick who found his tongue first. 'Guy Court,' he explained, 'is Freeland's Executive Director for Marine Safety. He visits all our ships, from time to time, to run drills, give seminars on the latest developments. Other companies use him as well as a consultant and trouble-shooter. He's a naval architect and engineer by training—in fact, he designed the *Enterprise*. He usually schedules his inspections in advance, but he also . . . drops in, as I guess you've gathered.'

'But I still don't understand,' Sarah persisted.
'If his presence will be so disruptive, why doesn't
someone from Freeland's management forbid it
just this one time?'

'Captain Court has complete freedom of movement on all our ships—he doesn't really report to
anyone. It was felt that in this way he could
maintain complete objectivity and the highest
standards. And anyway, Captain Court is. . . .' He
looked up, distressed, and his voice petered out.

'What Mr McQuade is trying so tactfully to
say,' cut in Tony, 'is that Guy *is* Freeland management, although his name is different from
mine. He's my cousin. His mother, Diana, is
Uncle Julian's youngest sister. Aunt Diana never
took an active role in the company, the way Julian
and Charles, my late father, did. Guy assumed
her position, just as I did my father's.'

'Oh,' said Sarah quietly, 'I see . . . I see.'

Darkness had blanketed the sea. Only the running
lights, twinkling in the distance, indicated the
point where the bow sliced steadily through the
water. The bridge was lit by the pale red of the
night lights. Sarah leaned back against the chart
table and watched as the navigation officer studied
the quivering blips that moved ceaselessly across
the radar screen.

Suddenly he turned to the Master. 'Radar
shows aircraft approaching from the north, sir,'
he said.

'Very well. Dead slow, helmsman,' Captain Price ordered. And to the duty officer: 'Floodlights on the landing pad, please, and prepare to assist the pilot.'

Sarah straightened and walked to the windows. In the distance, a pinpoint of green light blinked. If she hurried, she could make it to the deck that hung over the circular pad. Pulling her raincoat about her, she slipped out on to the open bridge and quickly scampered down the steps.

On the lower deck, she stopped and went to the rail. In the intense white glare of the lights the helicopter grew large, its lights flashing and jet engines screaming. For a brief moment it hovered above the giant bulls-eye, then dropped with amazing gentleness and precision to the deck.

Sarah clung to the rail as a blast of air from the throbbing rotors pushed her back, whipping her hair wildly about her face. With the jets still whining, the side door slid open. A figure jumped out and, bent low to avoid the slicing of the blades, ran quickly off the pad. He clutched a briefcase under one arm and was followed by a scurrying crewman carrying a suitcase and duffle bag.

As soon as the two were safely clear, the motors rose again to a deafening wail. The helicopter climbed steeply, swung sharply away from the *Enterprise*, and was rapidly swallowed by the night.

Sarah stood on tiptoe on the first rung of the

railing and strained to catch a glimpse of the new-
comer who stood directly beneath her, shaking
hands with Patrick. Their words did not rise to
her, but in the floodlights, the man was clearly
visible. *This* member of the Freeland clan, unlike
Tony, was in uniform—the full dress blues with
cap and gold trim that identified him as a senior
officer.

Sarah frowned as she studied his features,
deeply shadowed in the harsh overhead beams.
Part of his face was obscured by the peak of his
cap, but the strongly defined nose and jaw were
striking. A slight brutalness in the features seemed
at odds with the refinement of the uniform. This
contradiction between face and clothes was
vaguely familiar to her. Hadn't she seen that stern
profile somewhere else?

Of course! she thought, with a gratifying flash
of recognition. In the *Herald*'s file room . . . the
picture of the Freeland executives at the contract
signing. He had been the scowler in the back row.
Then, too, the ruggedness of the face had seemed
at war with the expensively tailored business
suit. Sarah extended her lower lip in a thoughtful
pout as she studied him. Evidently venomous
looks were a permanent characteristic of the man.

Sarah's impractical dinner shoes skidded on the
mist-slicked rail. Struggling to keep her balance,
she jammed her foot against the bar, and the delicate spike heel snapped, falling to the deck below
and clattering to a stop in front of Guy Court.

'Damn!' she said into the startled silence. She held her breath as he stared down at the ridiculous little thing at his feet. Wordlessly, he bent, picked it up, and turned it over in his large hand. Slowly he tilted his head back and saw her. His eyes held hers in a cold and strangely knowing gaze.

Sarah felt her heart thud.

He slipped the heel into his pocket and was gone.

CHAPTER THREE

IF Sarah had hoped to find an angle for her story by cornering Guy Court for a quick interview, she was disappointed. The second day out, he did not even present himself in the wardroom for meals. She caught only brief glimpses of his back as he strode down corridors, or a shock of dark hair as he vanished down stairwells.

The rest of the *Enterprise*'s crew were frustratingly inaccessible as well. And you didn't have to be a reporter to figure out that the reasons for their sudden withdrawal and the tension that seemed to grip all of them was Captain Court. Sarah found this intensely irritating. When Tony, the man in *charge* of the project, was so generous and helpful, how dared this interloper descend on them with his disturbing influence!

Sarah set aside her notebook on the chartroom table. She was impatient with herself for what she had to concede was an over-reaction to a man she had yet to meet. There had been only that one unfortunate look exchanged the day before. That, of course, had chilled her. But it was hardly a sufficient basis on which to form an opinion of the man. Had he assumed she was one of the officers' wives? If that were the case, he had been particularly rude.

She walked across the bridge room to the broad, slanting windows. They had left the main shipping lanes far behind and were running up the west coast of Greenland, in the safest, ice-free route. The sea ahead of them was deserted, sunlit, and intensely blue. The purity of the light was glorious. Sarah stared dreamily out the window and did not hear them until they were directly behind her.

'Sarah—I've been hoping we'd run into you!'

She turned, and was face to face with the two of them. For cousins, they could not have been much more dissimilar. Both were tall, it was true. And they were close in age, although Guy, she judged, was the younger. But while Tony was all polish, refinement, and dark good looks, Guy was a man of barely restrained power and hard, almost brutal lines.

The old saying was quite true, she thought, astonished at the jolt of her own response: a uniform did amazing things for the male body. There was something unsettling about the breadth of navy shoulder, the snow white shirt, the precision and gleam of gold embellishment.

But despite the impeccable grooming, the strongly muscled frame still looked about to burst out of its starched and well-cut confines. He was without cap, and a shock of thick dark hair slipped rebelliously down one side of the broad forehead. The strong nose and broad, high cheekbones bore the permanently ruddy colour of a face more accustomed to the deck than the boardroom. The green-flecked eyes threw a look at Sarah that was shockingly cold.

Tony began the introductions, but was cut off sharply. 'Yes,' said Guy, without a hint of cordiality, 'I know who Miss Grey is—the Canadian reporter you've hired.'

'Not hired, no,' Tony corrected immediately. 'Invited, is more like it. Sarah is strictly in the employ of her newspaper.'

'Of course,' amended Guy. 'My mistake.'

But his apology, Sarah sensed, was laced with sarcasm. She felt her body tense instinctively and self-protectively. With an effort, she forced herself to smile evenly and look unblinkingly into the uncomfortably clear green eyes.

'Your arrival has created some excitement on board, Captain Court,' she said with unfelt brightness. 'I know you're busy, but I'm hoping you'll be able to find time to answer a few questions.'

'On or off the record?' he replied, his voice very near a sneer.

'Why . . . on, of course,' she managed to say, thrown completely off balance by his baffling sarcasm.

Tony was suddenly edgy and his eyes darted from one to the other. 'Guy should have lots of free time very soon,' he said quickly. 'So far he's found everything running beautifully—up to or exceeding Freeland's standards. Isn't that right, Guy?'

'Yes,' he conceded shortly.

Sarah began to feel profoundly irritated by this sour man.

'Guy will be far too modest to tell you himself, Sarah,' Tony continued smoothly, 'so I'm forced to do his bragging for him. As you know, an ice-breaking L.N.G. carrier is a new creature on the seas. The *Enterprise* was conceived by Guy and built largely from his own original designs.'

'Oh?' said Sarah lightly. 'That *is* impressive.' Darn, she fumed silently. She *was* impressed, but part of her didn't want to let Guy Court know. Still, her voice had been much chillier than she had meant it to be. Better sit on those feelings! she told herself sternly. To return to antagonism emanating from him would be cutting off her nose to spite her face.

She felt her admiration for Tony growing steadily. A lesser man might begrudge giving up any of the glory associated with the *Enterprise*. His graciousness was particularly winning since his cousin hadn't even had the courtesy to tell him he was planning to accompany them.

The duty officer popped his head out of the chartroom and beckoned to Tony. Dismayed, Sarah found herself alone with Guy . . . and an appalling silence. She had to fight back the urge to walk out on him.

What she really needed to do, she thought, was

to retrieve her position with him by saying something terribly intelligent and technical, something that would shatter this man's smug sense of superiority. Maddeningly, nothing but inane generalities came to mind. And to make things worse, she felt he was watching her, somehow understanding her dilemma. She could summon nothing but a tiny, twisted smile.

Guy Court lounged lazily against the window, his head cocked to one side, a self-satisfied smile turning up one corner of his mouth.

'So,' he drawled, 'Tony's girl reporter is off on an adventure and wants to spin tales of life on the high seas. I'll bet I can guess your lead: the size of this vessel staggers the imagination ... stood on end, it would be taller than the Empire State Building ... and you'll close with rave reviews of the chef's marvellous menus. Really, Miss Grey—you didn't have to go to these extremes to get your story. Titbits like that are readily available from Freeland's public relations department.'

Sarah winced, having made just such notes in her cabin that morning. It was like a slap in the face, and for a moment she was stunned into silence, the sharp retort she wanted to deliver choked off in her throat. Perhaps it was just as well, she thought grimly. The brisk, efficient bridge was hardly the place for the tirade bubbling impotently inside her.

Recovering, she replied as calmly as her thudding heart would allow. 'If details like that help my readers visualise life on the *Enterprise*, I won't hesitate to use them. But I respect the public's intelligence too much to give them nothing but trivia. I'm a *science* reporter, not a travel adviser. So I repeat: I would still very much appreciate the chance to interview you on the safety aspects of L.N.G. carriers.'

'Oh, I'm all for that,' he replied sardonically. 'We could begin by advising against the women on board wearing silly spike heels.'

Sarah felt an unwelcome flush spread across her cheeks. 'I'm sorry about that,' she said. 'I'd just come from the Master's first night dinner. As you can see,' she added gamely, looking down at her sensible walking shoes, 'I'm better equipped now.'

His eyes travelled down her slowly, from the trim, beige cashmere turtleneck to the smooth leg of her brown tweed pants. Acutely uncomfortable, Sarah rushed on, 'Do you think we could set up a time now?'

He hesitated, then shrugged carelessly. 'I'm on my way now to meet the senior officers. I don't know how much of it you'll understand and frankly, I don't have the time to explain it to you. But if you'd like to sit in, you may.'

Once again Sarah found herself choking on his condescending manner. She was beginning to loathe the man, but the professional in her rallied. 'Yes,' she said, her eyes meeting the challenge in his and refusing to waver, 'I'd like that very much.'

Guy sat at the head of a long boardroom table, piles of charts and graphs and computer print-outs before him. There were no preliminaries. He sliced immediately to the business at hand.

Ruefully, Sarah had to admit that he displayed a stunning depth of knowledge that she, even with her string of degrees, was hard pressed to begin to keep up with. His was such a field of extreme specialisation. There could not be more than a few—perhaps even none—who would be his equal in the world.

'A ship this large,' he was saying, 'with a cargo this dangerous, can't help but be difficult to handle. All the mechanical marvels in the world can't make up for a crew which is not trained or sufficiently caring. If we allow ourselves to relax, to become complacent, it won't be long before we have a real disaster on our hands. It could start with something as simple as a man lighting a cigarette in a restricted area, or as complex as the breakdown of a sophisticated piece of equipment.'

His comment rang a bell in Sarah's head. Startled by her own audacity, she waved her pen and caught his eye. He raised an eyebrow.

'A question, Miss Grey?' he asked with exaggerated politeness.

Sarah inhaled deeply. 'Yes. About all this new equipment. Do you have the capability to repair

it on board, or would the breakdown on a critical
piece incapacitate the ship?'

'Miss Grey has immediately sniffed out our
Achilles heel, gentlemen. This is indeed one of
our worst problems. Very few shipyards are qualified to repair super-tankers. And most of the ones
that are would probably refuse us entry if we were
crippled and fully loaded with L.N.G.'

Tony, who had remained aloof throughout the
meeting, suddenly sat upright and cut in impatiently. 'I think you should make it clear to
Sarah, Guy, that our technical crew is superbly
trained—largely, by you! And we carry most critical components in duplicate for the rare event of
a breakdown.'

'Most,' agreed Guy slowly, 'but not all. As you
know, Tony, if I had been consulted, I would
have recommended a delay in the *Enterprise*'s
departure until we'd finished training that would
have made us almost entirely self-sufficient.'

'There's that "almost" again! No one knows
better than you that a guarantee of total safety is
simply not possible. We're not gods, Guy, only
men who try our damnedest. What do you want
of us?'

Unexpectedly, Guy retreated a little. 'Well, it's
done, and we're here. And every minute takes us
deeper into the Arctic . . . and into winter. So, if
Miss Grey has no further questions, perhaps we
can proceed with an outline of the program I have
mapped out for us.'

His catalogue of possible catastrophes was spine-chilling, exceeding anything Sarah had read. So super-cold was the L.N.G. that even the smallest leak from the cryogenic tanks would crack open the steel decks like an egg. Heavier than air, it would flow rapidly across the ship and out over the water, instantly freezing and killing any life it touched. The surface of the sea would freeze and erupt in a violent mixture of ice crystals and noxious vapour.

If the very worst happened and there was an explosion, it would have the force of an atomic bomb, shredding the massive steel hull. Everything for miles would be incinerated in a giant fireball that would create winds of hundreds of miles an hour. Nothing would survive it.

At least, that was one theory. No one knew for sure what would really happen. So far in history, there had never been an explosion of a L.N.G. super-tanker. But the threat was to be a constant companion of everyone on the *Enterprise*.

'We would be fools,' said Guy, 'to think our luck will last for ever.'

'But, sir,' interjected Patrick, 'it's not really luck at work here, is it? You yourself hand-picked this crew. I think we've left very little to chance!'

Sarah cast a discreet glance down the table to Tony, who was nodding in silent agreement with the First Officer.

'Perhaps you have more faith in men than I do,' Guy offered. 'Men are fallible. Nothing will ever change that.'

'Then what's the answer, sir?'

'There is none. There's only training and drills and above all, discipline. To that end, I will be holding a series of drills to simulate various emergencies we might run into. Some will be announced beforehand, some not. In any event, your men must act as though each exercise is the real thing.'

Angus Dunn, the First Engineer, was frowning and biting on the stem of his pipe. Guy was quick to catch his perplexity. 'A problem, Mr Dunn?'

'Maybe. My men in the engine room are tense enough, trying to get the feel of this new equipment. I'm picking up an atmosphere down there I'm not happy with. I'm wondering—only wondering, mind you—if your constant inspections aren't going to cause some trouble.'

Guy looked around the table. 'How do the rest of you feel about this?'

'I've seen it, too, sir,' said Patrick cautiously. 'Nothing I can pin down, yet. Just a general tenseness.'

Tony's hand suddenly came down on the table with a slap that made Sarah start. 'This is exactly what I was afraid of, Guy. Why couldn't all this have been done while they were on sea trials from Japan to Rotterdam? These scare tactics of yours are demoralising the crew. They're a fine bunch of men, and they deserve better than this!'

Sarah set her pencil down and folded her hands in her lap. If Tony and Guy were going to air some dirty Freeland linen, she didn't want to be caught writing it down.

'That had been my intention, Tony,' said Guy with deceptive calm. 'You know very well that I had no choice but to accept the S.O.S. from that tanker breaking up off South Africa. It threatened to give us the worst oil spill in history. You may recall that before I left I requested a delay in the *Enterprise*'s departure.' Sarah watched the rhythmic tic of a jaw muscle with growing alarm.

Tony jabbed a long finger angrily at the table. 'In the first place, you needn't have gone. You knew we were committed to this sailing date. Freeland Shipping does not go back on its word! Every day that goes by costs us a hundred thousand dollars, whether we're at sea or tied to a dock. Price was satisfied with her seaworthiness. I was not about to delay a multi-million-dollar venture just because you were off playing hero!'

It was far too intimate a baring of emotion between the two men. Sarah studied the faces of the officers. Each was flushed with embarrassment, staring at his pen or nails as if they were the most fascinating object in the world. Only tough old Angus Dunn was openly looking at Tony and Guy, obviously enjoying the set-to immensely.

'What I think is demoralising, Tony,' said Guy, through tightly clenched teeth, 'is facing the un-known. I want to be honest about what may be ahead. If you officers think I'm asking too much of your men, I'm sorry. But I've only just begun here.'

He gathered his papers, shoved them into his briefcase, and rose, all in one motion. 'Questions, gentlemen?'

The reply was an uneasy silence. He nodded abruptly and vanished.

Not half an hour had passed before the clang-clang-clang of the emergency alarm made Sarah's heart leap. The duty officer's voice broke over the loudspeaker. 'Fire in the engine-room! Fire in the engine-room! Emergency stations!'

Sarah heard the sudden banging of cabin doors and the thudding of dozens of feet in the corridor. Was it a drill, or was it the real thing? She felt the unpleasant surge of adrenalin pumping into her system and was sorry for the crew who had to respond with such absolute calm.

Sarah had heard the officers speculate that there would be at least one prearranged drill before Guy surprised them. She, however, guessed otherwise. If she was wrong, of course, if there really was a fire, she knew she would be breaking a cardinal rule and would, one way or another, be in a great deal of trouble. At the lifeboat drill, it had been stressed that she, Katie, and Emily, on hearing such an alarm, were to don their lifejackets immediately and wait in their rooms for further instructions.

But Sarah was determined to follow her hunches whatever the danger. In a flash, she was out of her room and racing down the steep steel steps to the engine-room.

The atmosphere was almost hellish with the ceaseless pounding of machinery, the steady whoop of alarms, and the flashing of lights. At first, the rush of activity in the windowless room with its banks of control panels told her she had made a fatal mistake. Intense concentration was painfully etched on the sweat-streaked faces of the men. Whatever was going on was being taken with dead seriousness. But there was no smoke, no fumes. And finally she saw Guy and Patrick, standing on a metal grid platform overlooking the scurrying troops. They held the ever-present clipboards and were taking notes.

Sarah exhaled with relief. She had guessed right. Now the problem was to find a safe niche where she could keep from being plowed under in the mad rush. And, she thought, with a tickle of apprehension, keep from being spotted by the formidable conductor of this exercise.

She scanned the room frantically, but was not quick enough. Guy had spotted her, and his anger was written clearly across his face. He slashed the air with a furious gesture indicating, she knew, the exit.

In return, she tossed him a quick wave and her brightest smile. With mingled fear and satisfaction she watched a thundercloud settle on his brow.

He shouted at her, but over the din she could not hear him. It didn't count, she told herself, that she knew from reading his lips that the words he spoke were quite to the point and perfectly clear: Get out!

Keeping her smile intact, she cupped her hand to her ear and shook her head to show she couldn't hear him. Then she made a dash for the corner and did not look at him again until she was sure he was too occupied with other matters to bother with her.

A young cadet went trotting up to him. 'Valves four and five will be closed next, sir,' he rapped out in obvious satisfaction with his role in the little drama.

'Correct,' came the reply. 'But valve five will stick, Grant. Your next move——'

The boy's face fell. He had not expected this imaginary complication. His eyes looked slightly frantic as he racked his brains for an answer.

'I will inform Mr Dunn, sir,' was his hopeful response.

'Mr Dunn has been overcome by fumes, Grant.'

Grant bit his lip in near panic. Confused, he

stared at Angus Dunn who, far from being overcome, was busy himself at a control panel. For a moment he looked utterly rattled, unable to sort out what was wanted from him. Sarah felt a wave of sympathy for him. There was no need to bully him! Even Patrick looked as if he was willing Grant to come up with the right answer.

'I'll shut down the control switch on the oil flow control panel, sir.'

It was more of a question than a statement, but the almost imperceptible upturning of Patrick's lips told Sarah he had acquitted himself.

'Carry on, Grant,' was all that Guy said. The cadet grinned and fled.

Not even a word of praise, thought Sarah, scribbling furiously. Did he always have to be so tough?

The klaxon became mercifully silent. The last of the imaginary flames were presumably smothered, explosion averted, and the mock injured carted out on stretchers. As Patrick instructed the crew to stand easy, Sarah executed her own departure.

She closeted herself in her cabin for the rest of the day, having the steward bring her dinner on a tray. It was almost bedtime before she was through. Pushing her chair back, she looked at the growing pile of paper with quiet satisfaction. Slowly, slowly, out of the great mass of data she was collecting, she was beginning to fashion a first-rate story. The real thrust of it she did not yet have a feel for. But she trusted it would come, in its own good time.

Exhausted from hours spent bent over her desk, sticky from the heat and chaos of the engine room, she craved a long, hot shower.

An hour later, wrapped in her silk dressing gown, a towel circling her damp hair, she padded back into her bedroom. She glowed from head to toe from the stinging spray, and smelled delightfully of powder.

There was a single knock at the door, Katie, she thought, crossing barefoot to the door. It would be lovely to curl up and chat with another woman after such a difficult day!

But the face that greeted her was Guy's, and without invitation he pushed past her. Sarah shrugged. 'Do come in,' she said to his back.

He didn't reply, but looked openly around the cabin, sauntered over to the desk, and flipped carelessly through her notes.

Sarah put her hands to her hips and stared at him in disbelief. 'Do you *mind*?' she said, exasperated. 'That happens to be my private work!'

He looked at her coldly. 'I see,' he said, a hand thrust aggressively into his pocket. He had taken off the uniform and replaced it with slacks and a heavy turtleneck. 'Intruding on other people's work is strictly a one-way street with you.'

Sarah folded her arms defensively across her chest. 'Tony didn't put the engine room off limits to me, you know.'

'And *you* know I specifically ordered you out of there this afternoon!'

'There was a great deal of noise in there,' she retorted.

'Don't play games with me, Sarah. I'm not that sort of man.' It was the first time he had ever called her by her given name, and it made her stomach do a curious little flip.

'I hadn't thought you were,' she replied honestly.

There was silence between them, painful and awkward for her, but seemingly of no importance to him. With maddening calm he lit a wooden match with his thumbnail and drew his pipe to life. Sarah inhaled the rich, stirring aroma of his tobacco. Unsettled, she broke the silence.

'Would it be too much for you to tell me just why you've granted me this visit?'

'Two reasons,' he said at last. 'One is to return this to you——' He produced her broken heel which he tossed on to her bed. 'The other is to give you a little free advice. Be careful about what you write, Sarah. You're in way over your head here, and you can do a great deal of damage through ignorance. So do everyone a favour and stick to chatty descriptions of lifeboat drill, or how the officers' wives pass their time.'

'You know,' she said softly, 'you really are insufferable. What gives you the right to speak to me this way? To assume that you know what I can and cannot write!'

His voice was deep and disturbing. 'There isn't any point in trying to deceive me, Sarah. You know as well as I do what I'm talking about.'

How could she argue with such vague and malicious insinuations! Helpless with frustration, her breasts rose and fell with each angry breath. Was it utterly beyond him to be civil to anyone?

She saw his eyes fasten on the damp tendrils of hair that clung to her cheeks. Indignantly she watched as he turned and eyed the array of cosmetics on her bedside table. Insolently, he picked up a tiny crystal flask of perfume and bounced it on his palm.

'I think you'd better go now,' she flashed, yanking the door open.

'Right,' he said. 'It looks as if I've interrupted some preparations. Primping for a nightcap in the owner's suite?'

The fragile control Sarah had fought for snapped. Her hand came across his face with a force that shocked her. Inhaling sharply, she clutched her smarting fingers to her chest and watched the ugly scarlet mark that sprang up on his cheek.

Incredibly, there was no response from him. He simply turned calmly on his heel and left her room as if absolutely nothing unusual had happened between them.

Sarah slammed the door shut and fell back against it, weak and trembling. Anger and guilt in equal measure churned inside her. Guy Court had radiated contempt for her from the first time he had laid eyes on her. Now she thought he actually hated her. It was insane. Nothing could explain such an unreasonable dislike between two people!

The drowsiness that had fallen over her earlier evaporated, and the cabin began to press in on her from all sides. Quickly she rubbed her hair dry, pulled on pants and a sweater, and headed for the distraction of the wardroom.

Sarah discovered that the wardroom of a super-tanker never closed down. It was always available as a hushed and comfortable haven for those who must work while the rest of the ship slept. Huge urns dispensed a steady stream of coffee and chocolate for those coming to or from watches, while a buffet provided an array of sustaining cold meat, rolls and fruit.

As Sarah slipped in, she was delighted to see the welcoming face of Emily Price. 'Sarah, my dear—come and join me! I'm just putting in some time with coffee and the latest thriller until John comes off duty.'

Sarah got her own mug and settled down beside the older woman. 'I didn't know Captain Price worked this evening shift, Emily.'

'He doesn't, usually. But there are standing orders to summon him when we run into fog.

We're into quite a patch of it now.'

For a while, the two women talked companionably about Emily's life as a Master's wife. The muffled throbbing of the giant screws far beneath them and the pale circle of amber light that encircled them had a tranquillising effect on Sarah. But perversely, she found herself looking for an opportunity to bring the conversation around to Guy Court.

'Do you know Tony and Guy personally, Emily?' she asked at last, nervously running a long, polished nail around and around the rim of her mug.

Emily set her empty cup on the table and frowned. 'Since boyhood, I suppose,' she replied. 'But only from a distance . . . more through company gossip, you might say. John knows Guy very well, though, and I've come to know him better since I've been going to sea myself.'

'But not Tony?'

'Oh, no,' she replied, shaking her head emphatically. 'Tony never sailed the way Guy did. There's one thing you have to understand about those two: they both share one obsession in life, and that's Freeland Shipping. They've lived and breathed it since they were in short pants. But from entirely different perspectives.' Emily paused and tilted her head thoughtfully. 'It's as if when they look at a ship, they each see something else.'

Sarah tucked her tiny feet up under her and

leaned closer to her companion. 'How do you mean, Emily?'

'Well . . . I think Guy sees only the ship—its design, its structure, its personality. But Tony sees it as just one part of the whole . . . something that serves the entire shipping enterprise.'

'I suppose they both began to work early in the family business.'

'That's true,' Emily confirmed. 'But once again, in very different ways. You see, the business came down equally into the hands of the three Freeland children—Julian, Charles, who was Tony's father, and Diana, who is Guy's mother. Several years ago, Charles was killed in an automobile accident. It was at that point that Tony began to take an active role in the administrative side.'

'That must have been a relief for Julian.'

'Yes, I think it was. He and Charles were very close, I understand, so it did his heart good to see Charles' son step in.'

'And where did that leave Guy?'

'Well, Guy, you see, was never one for the landbound side of it. By the way, Tony and Guy both have brothers and sisters. But none of them wanted to work in the business, although they all retain some financial share in it. Anyway, when Guy was still in his teens, he went off as a deckhand and learned every phase of a ship's operations. For a while there I think Diana Court was fretting that she was going to have a son on her hands with no formal education to his credit. But eventually, in his twenties, he went back to school in England and took advanced degrees in marine engineering and architecture. He developed a special interest in the safety problems on super-tankers. Right about that time there was a string of very bad accidents—oil spills and explosions. Lives were lost, fisheries ruined. They *weren't*, I should add, Freeland ships.'

'Yes,' said Sarah, 'I recall them very well. The pictures were terrible . . . beaches ruined, black-ened seagulls trapped and dying. And fishermen who'd spent their lives paying off their boats—bankrupt!'

Emily pressed her mouth into a thin line. 'It was a terrible business, all right. And it was in response to it that Julian established Guy's office as Executive Director of Marine Safety. It caused quite a stir at the time, I remember! But John was all for it.'

'Not everyone agrees with your husband, I take it.'

'Sorry to say, no,' conceded Emily. 'Guy's authority causes some to fear him . . . maybe with reason, who knows? But still, he's in great demand. Other shipping companies call him in frequently as a consultant, sometimes too late, and then he has to figure out what went wrong. If the proper systems for coping with a problem don't exist, then he's back at the shipyards designing them.'

Sarah gave a quirky little smile. 'He's quite a man, then . . . architect, lecturer, engineer, a general gun-for-hire.' And, she wanted to add, a boor and a bully who was far too sure of himself. She settled for a more diplomatic tack.

'Still, his purpose would be better served if he didn't come on quite so strong, don't you think, Emily?'

Emily chuckled. 'Maybe it's all that time at sea. It encourages a kind of directness in a man. And Guy never was one to hold back. Not like Tony, who has those smooth-as-cream manners . . . although I hear there's a good bit of iron there, too. Rumour has it,' she added, inclining her head to Sarah's ear, 'that the contract for the *Arctic Enterprise* just about split the company down the middle.'

Sarah blinked. 'But why would such a goldmine cause friction in the company?'

Emily shrugged. 'No one knows for sure. Being a family-owned business, they can keep secrets better than most. But it's thought that Guy dragged his heels and almost cost them the contract. Tony fought—and won. In the bargain, he supposedly pulled Freelands out of financial hot water.'

Sarah shook back her auburn hair, incredulous. 'What would he have to gain from undermining his own company? It doesn't make sense!'

'Oh, mind, I'm not saying he did. Some say

he was using the *Enterprise* as an excuse to ex-
ecute some sort of power play for control of the
company, but made a serious mis-calculation.
People have always thought that Guy would
emerge the stronger of the two and eventually
dominate the company the way his Uncle Julian
did for years. Now they're wondering. If there
was a power struggle, I'd say Tony's been the
victor.'

Sarah bit her lower lip softly, lost in thought.
'Emily,' she said at last, 'could it be that Guy is
putting everyone through this harrowing inspection just out of spite . . . to take some of the glow
off his cousin's triumph?'

Emily looked very stern. 'I won't believe that
of Guy,' she said firmly. 'Not without proof. I've
never thought he had a devious bone in his body.
Oh, he may run a little roughshod over people
sometimes. But it would be a bitter disappoint-
ment to find out he's capable of such mischief!
But now, Sarah,' she said, her voice brighter, 'I'm
afraid I've overstayed myself. John will be wondering where on earth I've wandered to! Will
Katie and I see you for breakfast in the morning?'

Sarah started, drawn abruptly from her
wandering thoughts. 'Oh yes—bright and early!'
she chirped. She waved goodbye as Emily
trundled out of the door, but her mind was
already spinning off, trying to unravel the twisted
relationship she was beginning to perceive between the two cousins.

Emily obviously resisted the notion that Guy was a spoiler and a poor loser acting out of jealousy. But Emily had not seen the coldness in his eyes. Had not been the object of his vicious comments. She had. And she could believe him capable of anything.

The side door burst open, admitting a blast of newly frigid air and two junior officers. They looked exhausted and took no notice of Sarah as they filled mugs and brought them back to a corner table.

As he sat, one of them spilled scalding coffee on his uniform and said a short, unpleasant word.

'Easy, Mark,' said the other.

The young man sat down heavily. 'Sorry. I'm a bit off tonight, I guess . . . all this extra bother with Court.'

'You can't let him get to you like that,' his companion cautioned. 'We're not even into the rough stuff yet. Besides, Court's bark is worse than his bite.'

'Maybe,' said Mark, unconvinced. 'But I still say Freeland's right—it's a bloody imposition. How can the crew function with Court breathing down their necks and second guessing them all the time? I tell you, Ian, it's no way to run a ship!'

'Relax, will you? It's the Master who runs this ship, and no mistake about it. If Court gets too far out of line, he'll come down on him—hard.'

Mark gulped his coffee. 'And that's another thing. We've got a real power triangle here—the Master, the safety officer, and the project manager. In the crunch, who's in charge?'

Sarah slipped unobtrusively out the door leading to the outer walkway. The fog had thickened dramatically. It curled over the rail and dropped heavily, swirling about her feet. The ship's lights were only weak smudges. Hugging her jacket to her, she breathed deeply.

There was a new smell lacing that of the salt air. It was subtle but unmistakable. Ice. For the first time, Sarah felt a nibble of true fear.

CHAPTER FOUR

As Sarah slept, the *Enterprise* turned west, away from Greenland, and into vast Baffin Bay, the start of the old Northwest Passage. She awoke to a new world of intense light and cold. A new excitement gripped the ship as well. Heightened alertness marked the watches, since not even the marvel of radio waves bounced off satellites could better a man's eye in scanning the horizon for icebergs.

To the north of them, icebergs the size of mountains were 'calving', sending hundreds of new icebergs off to sea. From time to time the distant thunderclap of a million tons of cracking, falling ice would reach their ears. The *Enterprise* began to roll.

They were not late enough into the season for the pack ice to have closed over the surface of the water, but the watch officers reported a dullness to the sea's surface that signalled the beginning of frazil ice, that first film of sludge-like ice crystals. Sarah reserved her thermal underwear for the return voyage, but broke out another layer of sweaters and her down parka.

The night they officially crossed the Arctic Circle brought a surprise. As the dessert dishes were being cleared, an abrupt dimming of the lights caused startled 'ahs' to erupt from the table.

The junior officers announced an entertainment to celebrate the historic moment. A gangly chorus line decked out in cut-up sheets and scraggly mophead wigs snaked into the dining room. The high kicking of the knobbly knees triggered a rain of hoots and whistles. Two stewards were next, with a slapstick routine that brought tears of laughter. There was a call for a song from Katie, who apparently had a reputation from a past voyage as a songstress.

She blushed scarlet to her roots, but the warm encouragement of the crew brought her hesitantly to her feet. Unaccompanied, her voice floated sweetly over the room, bringing dreamy smiles to the hushed group. In the dim light, Sarah studied the men's faces and felt a pang of sadness for them. They were so far from their homes and families, with so many uncertainties awaiting them. Katie was their tie to everything they loved and missed and worked for. Sarah joined the enthusiastic applause as a blushing Katie gave a little duck of a curtsy and scampered back to her chair.

The ceremony climaxed in the remarkable and reluctant form of Angus Dunn, drafted to act as the official greeter to the Arctic—a polar bear.

'Mind,' said Sarah, whispering into Tony's ear, 'it takes a little imagination to see him as a bear!' His costume consisted of a rather dingy set of long underwear haphazardly stuffed with pillows, a healthy dusting of flour on his face and rusty beard, and a circle of soot on his prominent nose.

He produced a stack of papers from a basket, certificates naming everyone crossing the Circle for the first time a Member of the Royal Order of the Blue Nose. From the three wildly protesting women, the bear first demanded a dusty, smacking kiss before relinquishing the prize.

Sarah laughed until her eyes were bright with tears. Flicking a tickly coating of flour from her flushed cheek, she triumphantly displayed her certificate to Tony. 'It says I've passed the gateway to the top of the world,' she read, 'and entered the land of icicles, blizzards, williwaws and a myriad snowflakes! And it's signed, "Boreas Rex, Ruler of the North Wind". What's a williwaw?'

'I don't know,' said Tony darkly, 'but it sounds perfectly dreadful. I'd stay away from it.'

'I intend to,' said Sarah, looking very grave. 'And I also intend to have this framed when I get home. It's better than a Pulitzer Prize . . . almost!'

Tony folded his arms on the table and leaned towards her. 'And this story you're doing on us. Is it going to be Pulitzer material?'

Sarah cocked her head and considered. 'That I can't say. But it won't be for lack of material if it isn't. My room's awash with notes.'

Laughter erupted farther down the table. Tony bent low over Sarah. 'I'd love to talk to you about

how you're getting along, but I think our chances
of getting any peace and quiet here are shot for
the night. Could you spare a few minutes in my
suite before you turn in?'

'I don't see why not. I doubt we'll be missed
much here.'

Tony held her chair back and draped her
sweater over her shoulders. Together they slipped
out of the wardroom unnoticed—or so Sarah
thought. But in the general confusion, she could
not see the eyes that had followed their every
move.

The steward left brandy and coffee and
departed silently. Dropping his jacket over a chair
back and undoing his gold cuff links, Tony joined
Sarah on the sofa.

'So,' he began, filling her glass, 'how have we
been treating you?'

Sarah saw Guy's face flash before her eyes, then
said firmly, 'Beautifully! Really, Tony, I can't
praise your people enough. Even Captain Price,
with all he has on his mind at the moment, has
taken the time to talk to me.'

'I'm glad,' said Tony, settling back with his
brandy. 'I was worried that . . .' His voice trailed
off and for once, Tony Freeland looked hesitant.

'Worried that what, Tony?'

He made an impatient gesture. 'I thought perhaps that bit of an explosion the other day in the
conference room might have put you off. It was
nothing, really . . . just the usual squabbling that

goes on in any family. But I shouldn't have subjected you to it.'

Sarah shook her head. 'Don't give it another thought, Tony, honestly. I understand that on any project as complex as this there are bound to be differences.'

Tony looked out at the velvety blackness beyond the windows. 'We're so terribly proud of this ship. It's been a long and difficult road we've travelled, bringing her from the dream to the reality. I don't want anything to spoil it now!'

Spoil, thought Sarah. That was just the word she had used in connection with Guy. But Tony was a doer, a builder. She liked that. How much damage could Guy do to him if he took it into his head to be really unpleasant?

It suddenly occurred to her that Tony had taken a great gamble in bringing her along. She could, if she were that sort, hold a very large stick over him. As outlandish as the thought was, she wanted very badly to reassure Tony that he had nothing to fear from her corner.

In a completely feminine gesture, she laid her fingertips on his wrist. 'I hope you don't think I'll be influenced by Guy's bluster. I'm quite capable of sorting out the facts from all his storm and fury.' And on impulse she added, 'All this has been quite a strain on you, hasn't it?'

He gave a short, almost bitter laugh. 'It shows, does it? It's been a tough year ... the rush to complete the *Enterprise* on schedule ... Uncle

Julian's health declining. That's been the worst, I think. He's a marvellous old man, Sarah—you'd love him.'

He shook his head wearily and leaned forward, resting his elbows on his knees. He seemed to be struggling for words that were painful. 'He hates to give up the reins, and I understand that. But there are some decisions he really shouldn't, and can't, make any more. It's certainly not made any easier for him when others encourage him to do more than he should.'

Sarah took a sip of her brandy and looked at him candidly. 'You mean Guy,' she said simply.

Tony lifted his palms in a gesture of frustration. 'He doesn't mean to, of course. But they share this "old salt" camaraderie: Uncle Julian served in the Navy during the war. Whenever Guy's in London, they get together at the Club and spin tales for hours. That may sound harmless, but it only seems to push Uncle Julian farther and farther into the past and away from reality.'

'Have you spoken to Guy about this?'

Tony raised an eyebrow and smiled crookedly. 'Guy,' he said wryly, 'is not the easiest man to reason with. But look—I'm sorry to have dumped all of this on you! You're very easy to confide in, you know.'

Sarah poured graceful arcs of coffee into thin china cups and handed one to Tony. 'It helps just to talk sometimes,' she said kindly.

'I hope you don't think badly of me, Sarah.

I'm the first to sing Guy's praises—he's tops in his field. But it's such a narrow one. Sometimes I think it gives him tunnel vision. He forgets about the rest of it: the scheduling, the payrolls to be met, the labour negotiations. There are hundreds of employees looking to us for their livelihood, and I can't forget that for a minute. If this voyage is anything less than an unqualified success, a lot of people are going to be hurt.'

Sarah's long eyelashes swept up and she found Tony staring at her intently. 'Is something wrong?' she asked, her fingers moving nervously to the fine gold chain that encircled her neck.

'Absolutely nothing. I was just wondering if you aren't some beautiful apparition ... like the mermaids who used to beckon to homesick sailors. You're the loveliest woman I've seen in a very long time.'

'You *have* been working too hard!'

'Don't ever undervalue yourself! You've got the entire wardroom giddy over you—no, don't laugh, it's perfectly true! Listen, Sarah,' he said after a pause, 'when we're through here, would you be my guest for a week or two at our country house? We're going to have so much to talk over.'

'Oh, Tony, I don't know. It sounds lovely, but ...' How was she supposed to handle this? She and Tony had developed a very pleasant, uncontrived relationship in the short time they had

known each other. But she certainly wasn't inter-
ested in making the leap from simple friendship
to any sort of intimacy.

'Don't tell me——' he said, 'there's some lucky
young Canadian counting the days until you set
foot on dry land again. There has to be.'

'No,' she replied with a bittersweet smile,
'there's no one special I'm going home to.'

'That's a mystery I won't question. But if
you're hesitating because you're afraid it wouldn't
be quite proper, let me reassure you. The country
house is for the entire family. It's a beautiful old
Queen Anne manor, Sarah, with acres and acres
of farmland and forests around it. It's always
bursting at the seams with hordes of Freelands
and Courts and their assorted offspring and friends
and dogs. There'd be nothing indiscreet about
your presence.'

'I never thought otherwise,' she said quickly.

'Then you'll at least consider it?'

'Consider, yes,' she said at last.

'I can't ask for anything more than that!' Tony
said warmly. He folded his hand over hers and
gave it a gentle squeeze.

He made no other move towards her and, for
that, Sarah was grateful. As charming as she
found Tony, she wanted no personal entangle-
ments to muddy the waters of her assignment.

Their hands were still lightly clasped when they
heard a knock and looked up to see the door swing
open. Guy walked in and tarred them both with

an expression that brought two burning spots of colour to Sarah's cheeks.

'Working late, aren't you?' he demanded.

Sarah withdrew her hand from Tony's and smoothed her skirt primly over her knees.

'May I?' he asked, indicating the bottle of brandy.

Tony gave an impatient flick of consent. 'What can I do for you, Guy?' he asked with ill-concealed impatience.

Guy lowered his large frame on to the arm of the sofa across from them. 'I'm going to take a work crew down into Tank One tomorrow, to have a last look at the welds and submerged discharge pumps. After that, they can start spraying the tanks with L.N.G. to bring their temperature down to the point where they're ready to accept cargo. I thought you'd want to know.'

'What difference does it make? I'm sure you'll do exactly as you wish.'

Guy shrugged. 'Only trying to be helpful.'

'You mean you can actually go down into those huge tanks? I didn't know that!' exclaimed Sarah, the embarrassment of the previous moment forgotten. 'Guy, could you arrange it so that I can come along, too?'

He looked at her, his eyes narrowing slightly, then gave his terse consent.

'Wait a minute!' Tony shot out. 'I thought that was considered hazardous duty.' Sarah raised her eyes questioningly to Guy.

'Some of the men don't like it because it's eerie down there, but it's not what I'd call dangerous. Anyway,' he added, tipping his head back and draining his glass, 'it's good honest work for a story.'

Cynically, he looked from Tony to Sarah. 'Main deck, Station One, seven a.m. sharp,' he snapped.

It never failed, she fumed. They had not once been in each other's company without the sparks. She pulled the blankets back with an angry snap, bounced into bed, and lay there, smarting with anger.

Intuitively she knew that Guy Court was a powerful and potentially dangerous personality. And for some reason he had targeted her for his hostility. But *why*, that was the question!

Did he resent her simply because of her sex? Women were traditionally considered bad luck on ships, and in some men the superstition lived on. And if Guy really was consumed with jealousy of his cousin, it was logical—if ridiculous—that he would associate her with the enemy. Certainly he had no respect for her intelligence or backbone. But that much she could do something about!

Sleep brought her no release from her outrage. She awoke tired and on edge, but no less determined to join Guy and change his obstinate mind.

They were steaming just south of Resolute, the

only settlement of any size for hundreds of miles. Sarah had always loved that name. It made her think of romantic sagas of adversity, isolation, and courage. As if to draw some inspiration from it, she squinted at the sliver of pale grey land that lay along the horizon. The sun had barely begun to tint the sky a watery pink. The entire landscape was so totally without warmth or movement that she felt chilled and turned her back to it.

The six of them were huddled together, feet braced against the sullen roll of the ship, slapping their arms to keep warm. If it weren't for her stubborn need to prove herself to Guy, Sarah would have fled inside long ago. Instead, she stood staunchly exposed to the cutting edge of the wind, her cheeks flaming. She looked tiny in the puffy parka, her face childlike inside the fluffy circle of fur.

Sniffling with cold, her hands clumsy in mittens, she struggled to make notes as Guy assigned duties to each of the men. He had made at least one concession to the cold, she noted, and put a down parka on over his sweater. But his head was uncovered and the wind tossed his hair about his broad forehead.

He looked at home on that heaving deck, she conceded grudgingly. The air of command about him was striking. While Tony, too, received deference from the crew, something else was reserved for this man. He belonged here. The sea had even helped form his face as well as his character, weathering his skin and chiselling little lines about his eyes and mouth. Against her will, she admitted that she was slightly in awe of him.

The hull inspection was the one duty hated by each and every man on board with something that bordered on the irrational. The descent into the dark, cavernous bowels of the ship made brave and sensible men suddenly uneasy.

The open hatch revealed a succession of twisting, backtracking steep metal staircases. They wound down in a dizzy spiral until they were lost in total blackness.

Guy posted one of the men at the hatch with a walkie-talkie so that the intrepid band of explorers would never be out of voice contact with the deck. The others were to proceed, single file, down the side of the internal pipe tower. Patrick would lead, with Guy following up the rear, behind Sarah. With the exception of Sarah, they all carried powerful lanterns and transmitters.

'Keep in line,' Guy shouted to her as they stood at the brink. 'Whatever you do, don't make any move away from the group!'

'You can count on it!' she shouted back over her shoulder. She gulped down a queasy rush of vertigo and disappeared into the hole.

Deeper and deeper they trooped, until the light from the hatch became only a distant star. The intermittent crackle from the radios became their only link with the outside world as the darkness closed over them.

The descent might have been spine-tingling, but it was at least interesting. The inspection work, in comparison, was long, tedious, and numbingly cold. To her annoyance, Sarah found that the tanks were more fascinating in theory than reality. She followed dutifully after the men, but there was little to see in the murk, and less to do. She was overjoyed when Guy gave the signal to start the climb back up.

They were half way up when the crewman ahead of Sarah dropped his flashlight. Muttering, he bent to retrieve it and, as he straightened, his head hit the handrail with a sickening thud. Dazed, he fell back against Sarah, and only Guy's quick grasp kept them from collapsing in a heap on the stairs.

'Sorry, sir,' the man said weakly. 'I'm okay now.'

'Take your time, Walker,' called Patrick from up front. 'That sounded like quite a crack you took!'

'No problem, sir!' he replied quickly.

Easy, thought Sarah. You sound rattled. And sure enough, once more he staggered and groped for the rail.

Patrick flashed his light down into the man's face, catching a trickle of blood glistening on his temple. 'Better get him up to fresh air, Guy,' he said, draping one of the injured man's arms about his neck.

'Right,' said Guy. Turning to Sarah he said

briskly, 'You won't be able to see very well with
the three of us jammed together. And I don't like
the idea of you fumbling behind me. Stay here,'
he ordered. 'I'll come right back for you.'

Panic rose in Sarah. 'No, Guy, please!' she
whispered hoarsely. 'I'll find my way!'

'I've got one problem on my hands,' he rapped
out. 'Don't give me two!' Strong hands gripped
her shoulders and pressed her down firmly on to
the grid landing. He found her hand and wrapped
it around the guard rail.

'There is nothing, absolutely nothing, that can
happen to you if you sit exactly where you are
and don't budge until I get back. You see that,
don't you?'

'Yes,' she admitted in a tiny voice. Then, not
wanting to delay the poor man's return to fresh
air, she said in a stronger voice, 'Go on—I won't
go anywhere, I promise!'

Perhaps he sensed her courage was a sham, for
as he stood, he gave her hand a quick, encouraging
pat. Soon he and Patrick, with Walker slumped
between them, receded from her sight.

The darkness and silence down there were
absolute, and a wave of disorientation threatened
to engulf her. She could not, she lectured herself
sternly, give in to any flights of fancy. That strong
metal platform was not about to let her go.

But dear God, I *am* afraid! she thought. She
was sitting in the belly of a super-tanker, hundreds of feet beneath the surface of an icy sea, at

the edge of a great black abyss. Gingerly she slid her fingers sideways until she came to . . . nothing. A drop straight down to—no! she thought. Don't do this. Fight it! But a prickle of terror was crawling relentlessly down her spine.

'Sarah? Sarah!'

He was coming down the stairs quickly, as if they were no more dangerous than someone's front porch steps. The beam of his light hit her. He knelt beside her, his eyes searching hers. 'Come on,' he said, cupping her elbow in his palm. His voice was firm but not unkind.

Sarah willed herself to move, but couldn't. To her horror she found her hand frozen to the rail, the one thing she felt was her slender tie to reason and survival.

Gently, but with no room for protestations, his hand sought out hers and broke her grip. Humiliatingly, she found herself reaching for him. She heard him sigh and knew he was exasperated, but he seemed to comprehend the depth of her fear. Wordlessly, he pressed her two hands to his chest and wrapped his arms about her, enfolding her completely. Thankful that he wasn't going to lecture her, she lay against him, listening to the rapid flutter of her heart.

When at last he felt her body untense, he said simply, 'Let's go now.'

He drew her to her feet and, keeping one arm protectively around her waist, climbed with her to the light above.

'They're makin' a big fuss over nothin',' said Walker, and Sarah thought him about to blush.

'It just makes good sense to stay down after a knock on the head, Mr Walker,' she said, smiling down at her hapless companion who lay tucked under a crisp sheet in the infirmary. 'Here,' she added, 'I've brought you some magazines from the library to pass the time until they release you.'

'That's very kind of you, miss,' he replied.

'Putting you back in the salt mines tomorrow, I hear, Walker. Is that good news or bad?' Guy appeared, his broad shoulders filling the doorway.

The man grinned. 'Strange as it may sound, I'd rather be up and workin' than stuck here on my back when I've got nothin' worse than a cut, sir,' he said.

'Perhaps that bump scrambled your brains more than we thought. It looks like the good life here to me . . . soft bed, meals on a tray, pretty girls hovering over you.'

'Well, now that you put it that way, sir, I guess I shouldn't complain.'

Sarah stared at the pleasure written clearly across the crewman's face as he grinned up at Guy. It was just a hair short of worship. Strange, indeed, since it was Guy who'd drafted him into such unpleasant duty.

'Glad to see you so well,' said Guy, leaning

down and laying a hand on the man's shoulder.
'See you for tomorrow's big docking, shall we,
then?'

'You can count on it, sir!'

They left the infirmary together and walked the
deserted corridor in silence, an uneasy truce
hanging tenuously between them. When they
came to the door leading to the flying bridge he
stopped. 'I was going out to smoke a pipe,' he
said. 'But it's blowing out there—I don't know if
you'll want to come.'

'Well . . . perhaps for a minute,' she said.

He slipped his hand under her elbow to help
her over the raised threshold and at once she felt
a deep, warm rush of pleasure. It shocked her,
not because she was totally innocent about sexual
stirrings, but because it came in response to a man
she found so objectionable in other ways. It was
unfair that he had the power to whipsaw her
emotions like this!

They walked out to the farthest side of the deck,
to the point where it hung out over the water
rushing by beneath it. The wind had risen and
Sarah snuggled deeper into her parka, her hands
burrowing into her pockets. Guy flipped up the
collar of his navy pea jacket as the wind lifted his
hair back from his face.

Sarah was acutely aware of his nearness, his
special male scent of tobacco and leather. Be careful! she warned herself. This is probably only a
lull in the hostilities. She tipped her chin and

looked up at the Arctic night. The air was cry-
stalline; the stars intensely bright, their brilliance
frozen in the lush, black sky.

'This is what you love best, isn't it . . . just
being here, at sea. The rest of the business, it
isn't you at all.'

He exhaled raggedly. 'That's partly true, I suppose. I do love it here. And I spend more time
than I like back at my desk. But I'm not com-
plaining about that. It's my way of trying to give
back a little of what the sea has given me. It's not
a debt that can ever be completely wiped out,
though.'

'Tony sees it so differently, I think. He . . .' In
the smoky light from the bridge room, she could
see him looking at her with disconcerting intensity, and her voice trailed off.

'Yes,' he said, 'Tony and I *are* different. You
won't find that the same tactics will do for both
of us.'

Sarah shook her head. 'I'm sorry, I don't see
what you mean.'

His voice was brutal. 'Come on, Sarah. You're
bright and you're beautiful . . . and you're a
woman. You know that Tony loves the chase, the
elaborate, flattering games. I'm much more
direct.'

He raised his hands and gripped the fox ruff
that circled her questioning face. Pushing it back,
he exposed her auburn hair. His two large hands
cupped the sides of her head, his thumbs sweep-

ing across her cheeks, lingering at the corners of her mouth.

Her lips parted in protest, but before she could utter a sound, he covered her mouth with his. Delight surged through her, spreading in a hot wave across her breasts and stomach. Weakened, she leaned against him, his hands slid supportively down her sides, pressing her hips against him.

But memories surfaced from below the sensual delight, memories of a hostile and scornful Guy Court. Sarah's mind fought the pull of her body. The cool and rational Sarah, the girl who would not be manipulated by any man, struggled for control. She pressed her hands against his chest and twisted her mouth free of his.

'Don't!' she whispered hoarsely. She inhaled sharply as his beard rasped painfully across her cheek.

He looked down at her, bullying amusement touching the corners of his eyes. 'You surprise me, Sarah. I didn't think you'd mind doubling your pleasure.'

Sarah flinched. 'That's the second time you've made a very nasty insinuation about my purpose on this ship!' she flared. 'If you have something to say, I wish you'd come right out with it!'

But her anger only seemed to increase his amusement, for he gave a snorting little laugh. Enraged, she taunted him with the only ammunition she had against him.

'You really *are* jealous, aren't you? You can't

stand it that Tony has this wonderful success on his hands! You'll do anything to ruin it for him, even if it means stooping this low!'

He regarded her disdainfully. 'Perhaps I was wrong about you. Perhaps you're not as experienced as I thought. That's quite a rattled response to a simple kiss.' He turned to go, then stopped and looked back at her. 'Don't stay out too long—the temperature's dropping fast.' Stuffing his hands into his pockets, he abandoned her.

Sarah squeezed her eyes shut in mortification. He was right, she thought miserably. It *was* only a single kiss. Why had she allowed herself to be so thoroughly unhinged by it? She had always thought of herself as so mature, so sophisticated, even though she had, long before, chosen not to sleep with the men she was involved with. She must have looked like a schoolgirl to him!

She slumped dejectedly against the rail, guilt forming an unpleasant little lump in her throat. Somewhere along the line, the control that she depended on had eroded. She had forgotten that the only thing that really mattered was the story. If she continued to let Guy get under her skin like this, she was going to abuse the trust that D'Arcy had given her.

Somehow she had managed to put herself squarely between two feuding men. And a very nasty spot it was. The *Enterprise* was a small, closed community. There was no place to hide, no way she could avoid Guy in the days ahead of

her. There was only one way to handle this inci-
dent. She would be pleasant but offhand with
him, she resolved. Guy Court was *not* going to
ruin this assignment for her.

CHAPTER FIVE

'GOOD morning.' Guy scraped back a chair at the breakfast table.

A murmur of greeting went around the table. Sarah squared her shoulders. 'Good morning,' she said, her smile bright but brief.

'We were just talking about Sarah's story,' bubbled Katie. 'Won't it be wonderful to be able to read about ourselves when we get home?'

Guy nodded politely, but was silent, and speared a broiled kipper from the platter.

'She's got nothing but praise for us, I hear,' added Tony, smiling broadly. They were going to dock at Melville Island slightly ahead of schedule, and that knowledge had put the *Enterprise*'s owner in an expansive mood. 'But that's no surprise, is it, Guy?'

'No,' Guy agreed instantly, looking directly into Sarah's eyes. 'Sarah's story has always been entirely predictable.'

Sarah laid down her fork. Well, *that's* damning with faint praise, she thought. People looked up, puzzled, and Tony began to speak. Guy was quicker.

'I mean,' he added easily, 'Captain Price is the best in the business, and his crew reflects that.

How could she help but be impressed by such a well-run ship?'

Again, the right words, but tinged with another meaning. Or was she only imagining it? Had she become so sensitised to the man that the most innocent comment had to be scrutinised for double meaning? The heavily fringed eyes studied him over the rim of her coffee cup until the sound of her own name drew her back to the conversation.

'. . . and although she hasn't given me a firm answer,' Tony was saying teasingly, 'I think I've just about persuaded her to spend some time with the family in England. I thought she might like to look over our operations in London first hand, perhaps talk to Uncle Julian at the country house.'

He looked at Sarah with eyes so full of bright anticipation and good will that she could not help but smile. What a joy it was next to the soured, cynical expression that so often masked Guy's face!

She hadn't been ready to answer him. And she had, in fact, been leaning towards a refusal of his invitation, sensing that by agreeing she was tacitly committing herself to more involvement with him than she was prepared for. But one look at the mocking glint in Guy's eyes, and the words spilled out.

'I've been thinking about your offer,' she lied breezily, 'and I've decided I'd love to go!

Something on the company background and its other operations make a super follow-up story.'

The steadiness of her voice astonished her, contrasting as it did with the uneven beating of her heart. She hit Tony with that smile of hers, and firmly avoided Guy's gaze.

Mercifully, the address system crackled to life, diverting the attention that this exchange had sparked. Docking procedures were about to begin, and all hands were to take up their positions. Standing in unison, the men took final gulps of warming coffee and departed, almost at a run. Only the three women remained, savouring a quiet moment before they, too, would crowd the rails.

Katie broke another muffin on to her plate, an impish grin crinkling her cheeks. 'Gosh, aren't you excited, Sarah? Mr Freeland's just about the most eligible bachelor in the country—I'm always seeing his picture in the magazines, showing him at all the big social events. Why, he even goes to royal weddings and things like that!'

Katie's youthful enthusiasm was infectious. 'Well . . . yes,' Sarah allowed. 'Tony says the estate is glorious. And the family, by all accounts, is pretty lively. I expect I'll have a good time.'

Katie pounced in triumph. 'If you ask me,' she said, heedless of the fact that no one had, 'this is just like an old-fashioned shipboard romance—in a very modern setting, of course?'

Caught off guard by Katie's directness, Sarah felt herself flushing. Emily came tactfully to the rescue. 'Now, Katie,' she chided gently, 'you're letting that vivid imagination of yours run away with itself again. Perhaps Mr Freeland's just trying to be helpful.'

'Perhaps . . .' was all Katie would concede. 'You'd never think he and Captain Court are related, would you? One charms you right off your feet, the other just bristles and storms. Patrick won't hear a word against Captain Court, you know, but sometimes he scares me half to death.'

'And sometimes,' agreed Sarah, 'he scares me, too. I'm surprised that Patrick's so loyal. From what I've seen, your husband's the one who's borne the brunt of all the extra work.'

'That's true,' said Katie, suddenly serious. 'I've seen almost nothing of him since we sailed. But Patrick says he never asks a man to do anything he wouldn't do himself, and that's the mark of a true master. Isn't that right, Emily?'

'Oh, yes! John lives by that rule. That way, if the worst should ever happen, the men will be steadfast. They won't balk when great demands are made of them because they know the Master is asking no less of himself.'

Sarah crumpled her napkin beside her plate and pushed her chair back. 'Well, you two can characterise Guy any way you want,' she said, 'but I still think there's a bully masquerading behind that spiffy uniform! I'm going to get my parka and go up to watch the docking. See you on deck!'

She waved and cantered out of the door, leaving Emily and Katie staring bemusedly after her.

A ship like the *Enterprise*, pushed by its own great weight, could travel three miles before an order to stop it would take effect. That was only one of a hundred details John Price had to keep in his mind as he shepherded his charge into the floating, barge-mounted dock. Here there was no Mr Danner to help him through treacherous currents and around hidden obstacles.

Her feet tucked into high shearling boots, a black wool watch cap pulled down over her ears, Sarah watched the painstaking process through high-powered binoculars. She had drifted down the rail from her two companions. Katie and Emily understood only too well the enormity of the problem their husbands were shouldering, and Sarah sensed their need to be alone with their thoughts.

The ice-capped shore that moved slowly up to meet them was rocky and forbidding, an unlikely site for an outpost of man's highest technology. But perched precariously on that hostile and desolate ground was a cluster of high-domed metal buildings forming a protective ring around the deep, ice-crusted inlet. The colony bristled with pipes, antennae and control towers. The outer circle of supply huts and dormitories turned their backs, like buffalo in a blizzard, on a vast, unforgiving landscape. Streaks of sharp, flint grey

rock broke through the loose, drifting curtains of
snow. Beyond, the snow plain was dotted by
mirror-like lakes of ice reflecting a pale, buttery
sun.

The intense cold had not deterred the ground
crew who had turned out in force to greet them.
They lined the dock, standing on the roofs of
sheds and on packing cases, craning their necks to
watch the acrobatics of the rope handlers sprint-
ing across the *Enterprise*'s bows. When the ticklish
business of docking was finally over and the landing ramp joined the two worlds, a tremendous
cheer rose up from them. Sarah moved agilely
among the throngs on deck, recording with her
camera the elated faces and the victory signs that
were flashed back and forth from land to ship.

There was a ceremony on the bridge during
which the terminal supervisor and Tony made
brief, flattering speeches, exchanged engraved
mementos, and posed dutifully for publicity
photographs. The whole thing, to Sarah's amaze-
ment, was over in minutes. The crews began at
once to transfer the liquid gas from the land storage tanks into the *Enterprise*'s holds.

Tony and Sarah were lounging idly in swivel
chairs, watching the loading technicians bent over
their computers.

'What did you expect?' he asked, a smile playing
about his lips as he studied her frown.

'Oh, I don't know . . . it was just so rushed,'
she replied. 'You'd barely shaken hands with Gus

Cameron when everyone went trotting off to work.'

'You're forgetting that hundred-thousand-dollar-a-day operating bill we face. Minutes count in this business—we still have a small fortune in construction fees outstanding. It wouldn't take much of a delay to put us in the red on this run.'

Sarah pressed her lips together and looked doubtingly at Tony. 'You'll forgive me if I'm a bit sceptical about that. You stand to make more money from one run of this single ship of yours than someone like me will see in a lifetime.'

'It's true that the profits from this contract could be phenomenal—but so could the losses. It's a terrific gamble we're taking. Besides, all this so-called profit that people ramble on about: it doesn't go into my pockets. It's ploughed right back into the company to build more ships. We plan to have half a dozen of these ice-breakers on the Arctic run eventually. Frankly, Sarah, I can't help but be a little resentful when people imply that we're lining our family pockets with this money. How many others would be willing to lay everything on the line the way we are?'

'Not many,' Sarah said soothingly. 'I can see that shipping is hardly a pastime for the faint-hearted.'

But Tony seemed not to be listening. His eyes were drifting absently over the room, his long fingers drumming on the arm of his chair. Sarah wondered if he wasn't faintly bored with the discussion of empire-building.

'Do you ride, Sarah?' he asked unexpectedly, his voice once again animated.

'What—you mean horses? No, I don't. Why do you ask?'

'I'm wondering how I'll amuse you when I get you to Fairfield. We keep horses there and I thought . . . well, never mind. What *do* you like to do in your spare time?'

Sarah put down her notepad and crossed her legs. 'Spare time seems to elude me these days,' she replied with a wry grimace. 'But I do love to ski when I can snatch a day or two.'

'We're out of luck there, I'm afraid. What else?'

'Well . . . walking, if that doesn't sound too tame for you. I'm an addict. I go for miles and miles if I can. I find some of my best ideas for stories come to me when I'm walking.'

'You're an easy woman to please. I approve of that. There's some beautiful countryside around Fairfield that we can amble through. Some charming villages as well. I was thinking I'd meet you in London, show you the offices. Then we'll take in a play or two, and a few good restaurants. Afterwards, we'll drive down to the house and unwind a bit with the family. Will that suit?'

'Perfectly. Who do you expect will be there?' she asked casually, although she was thinking uneasily about Guy.

'If we make it about a month from now, we'll

be close to the holiday season. The children should be out of school, so I'd wager you'll see a fair size cross-section of us. There'll probably be my older brother Simon, who's in banking in London. He and his wife, Nina, have five children, if you can believe it. And my sister Laura— she's a very contented wife, mother, and charity worker, who has her own sizeable brood.'

'Tony, good heavens, that's close to ... twenty! You certainly don't need another house guest!'

'Wait, I'm not through yet! That's just the Freeland side. There'll be Aunt Diana, of course, because she lives at Fairfield on a more or less permanent basis. I hear Guy's youngest sister Emma is coming. She has her heart set on conquering the London stage—she's working as an assistant wardrobe mistress right now, though. Emma never seems to appear with fewer than half a dozen starving, but decorative young actors and actresses in tow. And Guy's brother Nicholas should make it—he's a master at a small school and will be on break. He and his wife have a new son.'

'Tony, please—I'm staggered! I come from such a tiny, quiet family. I can't imagine how you all squeeze into one house!'

Tony laughed. 'With a great deal of noise and confusion. I promise you you won't be bored! Sarah, I just realised—your visit will bring us right up to Christmas. Is there any chance you could stay over?'

Sarah quickly shook her head. 'I'm afraid not, Tony. My parents really look forward to the holiday season, and they've only got me. I couldn't desert them. Even though I technically live at home, a lot of my assignments take me out of town . . . although not usually this far afield. We don't see that much of each other. That will probably continue for as long as I can foresee.'

'Is that the way you want your life to be, Sarah? One glamorous job after another, with half your time spent criss-crossing the country? It must be exhausting!'

Sarah pushed back a strand of hair that had slipped across her cheek. 'First of all, very few of my assignments are what you'd call glamorous. It's mostly just plain hard work combined with a lot of deadline pressure. But now's the time to do it. Now, while I'm free of personal commitments.'

'Then there'll be a place in your life for a family of your own.'

'Yes,' she replied, smiling. 'In its own good time.'

Sarah's attention drifted to the technicians who were punching data into the loading controls. Tony's pointed and personal questions made her uneasy, and she wanted to steer them back to neutral ground. She was also beginning to regret having let herself be stampeded into accepting Tony's invitation. It was getting much more complicated than she'd ever dreamed.

Diagrams of the *Enterprise*'s hull glowed on the computer screens. Pulsing lights indicated the opening and closing of valves, the speed of the flow into the insulated tanks. They would also indicate, instantly, any hazardous stresses forming in the tanks, or any imbalance of pressure between the ship and the loading terminal.

Suddenly there was a persistent buzzing from one of the panels, and a knot of technicians formed at once around a flashing red light.

'Excuse me, Sarah.' Tony stood and crossed the room in a few quick strides. 'What's the trouble?' he demanded.

The supervisor exhaled slowly. 'There's a snag in the flow, Mr Freeland,' he replied, raking his fingers through his hair abstractedly.

'How can that be—you've checked and re-checked the equipment every day since we left Rotterdam!' His voice was harsh and accusatory, and Sarah saw suddenly just how raw and close to the surface Tony's nerves were. She had misjudged him: he wasn't as calm and in control as she had thought. Troubled for him, she stood and went to his side.

'I don't think the trouble's with us, sir,' the man replied with deliberate calm. 'I'd say it's at the pumping station end.'

'You don't *think*! A fortune in equipment at your fingertips and that's the best you can do?'

'Mr Freeland, sir, we've just this moment seen the warning. If you'll permit me, I'll get on the line to the shore office and see what they have on it.'

Bravely spoken, thought Sarah, considering the poor man had an alarm screeching in one ear and the ship's owner shouting in the other. She suddenly had another vision of Tony Freeland, of a man who did not tolerate frustration very well.

Apprehensively, she watched him pace the floor with long, restless strides as he listened to the incomprehensibly technical conversation between the supervisor and his land counterpart.

Exasperated, he grabbed Sarah's arm, finally, and propelled her towards the door.

'Where are we going?' she panted, jogging after him.

'To the shore office!' he rapped out, his eyes straight ahead. 'If someone on their side is messing up, I want to know about it!' The Arctic air caught in Sarah's throat like a knife as they skidded unsteadily across the slick, frozen ground.

The workroom was cheerless and functional, crowded with a welter of desks and draughting boards. Sarah paced it restlessly, attracting the curious and admiring stares of the all-male staff. From time to time she glanced into Gus Cameron's glass-walled office, where a huddle of men bent over a pile of blueprints. Once, she saw Tony gesturing angrily. They were telling him nothing, apparently, to improve his mood.

As the minutes dragged by, she accepted a

paper cup filled with coffee from one of the engineers and sank dejectedly into a vacant chair.

The office door opened and Guy came out, closing it quietly behind him. He came and sat on the edge of the desk in front of Sarah.

'Looks as if we're in for a long wait,' he said.

'I gathered as much—do they know what the problem is?'

'More or less. One of the pumps is malfunctioning. But at least it's nothing to do with the *Enterprise*. Tony should be grateful for that much.'

Sarah turned her head and peered back at the office. 'He certainly doesn't *look* very relieved,' she observed.

'Well, the bad news is that we'll be tied up at least one extra day—and probably two.'

'Two days! I don't blame him for being furious.'

He shrugged. 'You have to expect a few bugs the first time through.'

Sarah shook her head and swirled the coffee around in her cup. 'I suppose you're right. But still . . . two days!'

'Think you can come up with some way to put in the time?'

She raised a neatly arched eyebrow. 'To tell you the truth, I don't know. I've pestered just about everybody for an interview. And there's just so much you can write about a completely automated pumping system.'

'Well, there's always the movie theatre,' he tossed out, shrugging his broad shoulders.

She gave a small cry of exasperation. 'If you think I've come all the way to the Arctic just to sit in a dark room and watch re-runs of last year's cinema spectacles, then you don't know me!' She strode to the window and stood with her arms folded across her bosom, looking hungrily out at the icy blue vista. Her natural curiosity was never still for a minute. 'I want to go exploring,' she announced.

He gave her a quick look. 'That's not your ordinary countryside out there you know.'

'I do know that! But it's beautiful, in its own way. I've read all my life about the mystery and grandeur of the Arctic. I just want to go out there for a while and ... and ... *experience* it!'

An idea formed in her mind. Ignoring Guy's cautions, she turned to the man at the next desk, who had been a reluctant eavesdropper on their conversation.

'Excuse me,' she said, 'but don't you and the other men ever get away from the station—sight-seeing, I mean?'

The man put his pen down and smiled at her, delighted with her attention. 'Yes ... some of the men like to go out and try to sight birds and animals. As a matter of fact, the last time they went out they came across a native hunting party that had set up a temporary camp not far from here. That's pretty rare for this area—they were really excited.'

'There, you see?' She looked at Guy, and turned to the other man. 'Do you think anyone might be going out either today or tomorrow?'

'I don't know offhand. But I could try to find someone to take you out on a short trip.'

'Could you? I'd be so grateful!' she exclaimed, her face lit up with excitement.

The man grinned. 'Hold on a minute,' he said, standing. 'I'll see what I can come up with.'

Sarah tilted her chin and looked triumphantly at Guy. Old movies, indeed!

But when the man returned, he was apologetic. 'Mr Cameron gave his permission, but I'm afraid I couldn't find anyone qualified to take you. Almost all the leaves have been cancelled while the *Enterprise*'s in port.'

Sarah's shoulders sagged. 'Darn,' she said, giving the desk a little slap.

She was conscious of Guy's eyes on her. 'Well, there's always the——' he began.

'No way!' she retorted. 'Look,' she said to the engineer, 'couldn't I strike out on my own for a while? I wouldn't go far, and I'd be very careful.'

He shook his head. 'I don't think so, Miss Grey. You wouldn't get far enough away from the compound to see much. Besides, we'd really hate to lose you!'

Sarah gritted her fine white teeth in frustration. Two more days of staring at the backs of computer technicians. It seemed like such a waste.

'This hunting camp,' Guy was saying, 'Is it far?'

'No . . . less than an hour by snowmobile.'

'And the terrain?'

'No problem. It's a pretty straight run along the shore.'

'If we left within an hour, then, we could still be back well before the early dark?'

'*We!*' shot out Sarah. 'What are you talking about?'

He ignored her. 'Do you think you could fix me up with a snowmobile—I'll clear it with the top.'

'No problem that I can see, Captain.'

The man excused himself, and Sarah turned on Guy, whispering furiously, 'Would you please tell me what it is you think you're doing?'

'Giving you your heart's desire, I thought. I'm going to take you on a little tour of the tundra. We might even see a polar bear—a real one this time.'

'And what makes you think I'd trust myself out there with you?' she demanded, jerking her head towards the frigid scene beyond the windows.

'If there's one thing I know about,' he said calmly, 'it's navigation. I've even done a stint in the Arctic with your own armed forces. What happened to the girl who was ready to go out on her own? Still, if you're afraid . . .'

'Not at all,' she snapped, shaking back her hair. But she did, however, look with misgivings at the closed door of the supervisor's office. Guy followed her glance.

'He'll be tied up with paperwork the rest of the day. I heard him discussing it with Cameron. You think he won't approve. Say so.'

'Don't be silly. How many times do I have to tell you that I don't answer to Tony for every move I make?'

'You're afraid of *me*, then.'

'Certainly not!' She met his gaze steadily. He was judging her again, she was sure of it. Then she recalled her resolve not to let her emotions, or Guy Court, get in the way of her work. If she turned up this chance to see something of the Arctic just because of him, then she'd be breaking that promise to herself.

Of course, there was always the possibility that Guy was making an honest gesture of reconciliation to her. Perhaps he regretted the angry words they'd exchanged. She looked hard at his firm mouth, his determined jaw, the clear green eyes.

'How soon did you say we could be back?' she asked.

'An hour there, an hour back, and an hour or so to look around . . . we should be in by early afternoon.'

'Let's get going, then.'

The arrangements took no time at all. Permission was granted, maps, a hot lunch, and suitable clothes assembled. Guy checked with the meteorology department and received a forecast of clear weather for the next several days.

Sarah stood at the storeroom door and looked across the courtyard at Guy. He stood astride a sleek black snowmobile, one booted foot on the starter pedal. She watched as he drew himself up and came down hard on it. The motor roared to life, and he swept forward in a broad circle to where she waited.

'Hop on!' he shouted over the buzz-saw whine.

She took one breath for courage, fastened the helmet strap snugly under her chin, and selfconsciously raised her leg over the seat.

'Hold on tight!' he ordered, reaching behind him and pulling her roughly to his back. Her hands slid around his waist, her thighs pressed the outside of his.

'No dogs?' she shouted in his ear.

'No, but you can still say "mush" when I start her up. I have great faith in your powers of imagination!'

Sarah yanked her hood farther down her brow, hunched behind the warming breadth of his back, and obliged. Slapping the clear bubble visor of his helmet down over his eyes, Guy waved to a small group of observers at the storeroom door, and gunned the motor. With an arc of snow spraying out behind them, they hurtled away from the camp.

CHAPTER SIX

AT first glance, the Arctic had a deserted appearance, but Sarah was soon aware of a rich profusion of life. The air held snow geese, ptarmigans, kittiwakes and murres. The land was home to the sleek white fox and the burly musk ox, and the sea sheltered walrus, harp seals, and the white Beluga whale.

Guy raised a plump, mittened hand from the controls and pointed towards the ice-dotted water. Far off shore, on a drifting floe, Sarah made out the powerful, slope-shouldered form of a polar bear, padding agilely on all fours.

She pressed her mouth close to Guy's ear. 'Are you sure we're safe? I've read they're pretty dangerous!'

His voice drifted back to her on the wind. 'Out there, on the ice, yes—they're ferocious. But they're timid on land and don't often venture on to it.'

The bear, as if realising it had a rare audience, reared like a stallion, raking the air with deadly claws. Sarah shuddered, grateful for the huge expanse of water that separated them.

Despite the ground crew's assurances that the weather was unusually mild for this time of year,

Sarah felt an alarming cold moving up her legs. A long orange star of sun streaked the sky and tinted the snow around them, but it shed no warmth, and the wind penetrated her parka mercilessly. By the time they spotted the dark curve of pebble beach that was their destination, she had begun to wonder at the wisdom of her decision.

Guy brought the snowmobile to a smooth halt beside a small snow shelter that sat on an icy rise overlooking the beach.

'Looks as if we're out of luck,' he said, lifting the helmet off his head. 'No signs of a boat down by the water. Either they're out hunting, or they've moved on.'

'Maybe they'll be back before we leave,' Sarah said hopefully. She winced as she dismounted cautiously and straightened her cramping legs.

Guy scuffed at a shallow footprint in the snow. 'Not very fresh . . . I'd say they've abandoned the camp.' He stooped by the snow block tunnel that led into the igloo. 'Hello?' he shouted. There was no reply.

'It was *still* worth it,' Sarah said stoutly, her breath misting the air. 'It's so awesomely beautiful here. I'm never going to forget this as long as I live!'

She stood at the brink of the rise, her hands shielding her eyes, and gazed out at the endless expanse of azure sea strewn with a thousand pure white floes.

He regarded her with narrowed eyes. 'You're

half frozen,' he said curtly. 'Let's get something warm into us.'

He retrieved the insulated food container the camp kitchen had provided. Side by side on the snowmobile, they broke off chunks of bread and sipped steaming mugs of soup. Slowly the food pushed the cold out of Sarah's body. She was well aware that they were just two fragile specks of life near the hostile top of the globe, but she had no sense of fear. She felt only peace and contentment, and a strange, overwhelming sense of belonging, as if time had suddenly ceased for them.

But it was evident to her that Guy did not share her mystical calm. He wolfed his lunch, giving distracted replies to her chatter, and searched the horizon restlessly.

'What's wrong?' she asked, hurt. 'Are you bored?'

'No, not bored . . .' He broke off.

'What, then?' she persisted.

He nodded towards the horizon which had taken on a pale, purplish tint.

Sarah stared at it, then turned her eyes back questioningly to his face. 'A storm?' she asked. 'But the forecast was for clear weather.'

'Storm patterns in the Arctic are extremely unpredictable. I think we'd be wise to cut this short and head back,' he said, already tossing his cup back into the case.

'Just one quick trip down to the beach, Guy— please? I want to gather some stones to take back.'

'Make it fast, then,' he said. 'I'll get us packed up.'

She scrambled down the slope to the inlet. The wind had risen perceptibly, and the sea had begun to swell rhythmically against the pebble beach with a soft, grinding noise.

She traced the perimeter of the cove, stooping to pick up the water-rounded rocks and run them through her fingers like worry beads. The austere beauty of that spit of stone, protruding from the ice, moved her in a way she found hard to define. She inhaled the perfect air as if she might absorb and hold on to some of the Arctic's essence.

For how many centuries had the sea battered this beach, polishing those hard stones? It was a lonely place, yet both man and animals had survived here, unique and irreplaceable. Would the *Enterprise* and others like her really be the death of all this? Having lived on the ship and shared the dreams of the men who guided her, she found that possibility almost unbearably painful. And yet . . .

'On the double!'

She turned her face inland and felt a stab of sharp, ice-flecked wind lash her cheeks.

'I'm coming!' she shouted. Lowering her head against the wind, she struggled up to Guy through the shifting, falling pebbles.

She found him bent over the radio that was sputtering to life. 'What's up?' she asked, rawhroated from the frozen air.

'Quiet!' he barked, as he flicked on the trans-
mitter switch. 'Are you absolutely sure of that?'
he shouted into the speaker.

A disembodied voice crackled over the air. 'I'm
sorry, Captain Court, there was no warning on
this one. It's just one of those isolated squalls.'

'How long before it blows itself out?'

'Not long . . . a few hours maybe. Radar shows
nothing backing it up. But even a short time puts
ou——'

'I know,' he said grimly, 'into dark.'

'Right, sir. We think your safest bet is to stay
where you are and head back in the morning.'

Sarah's mouth dropped open and she started to
protest, but Guy's raised hand stifled her.

'I've taken the liberty of discussing your situ-
tion with Captain Price,' the voice went on. 'We
understand you're experienced in Arctic survival.
I gather you've located the hunting camp and
protection's no problem.'

'Right on that—we're well sheltered.'

'There are ample emergency supplies in the
snowmobile, of course . . . we're *really* sorry about
this, Captain.' The man sounded embarrassed.

'It's no one's fault,' muttered Guy, rubbing his
and thoughtfully across his mouth.

'We'll see you in the morning, then, sir.' The
radio went dead, leaving nothing but the whine of
the wind.

The reality of their situation slammed down on

Sarah. 'This is insanity!' she blazed. 'We can
spend the night out here. We'll freeze to death!'

'Nothing so dramatic, my dear,' he retorted
'We won't be comfortable, but we'll make it.'

'But the visibility's still good—surely we ca
beat the storm back to camp in less than an hour

'Not a chance. A white-out could send us flyin
over an embankment and leave us bobbing in th
sea like a couple of ice cubes.'

Sarah stared at him through lashes that sparkle
with clinging snow flakes. 'But we *can't* spend th
night here! Not alone.'

'You don't have any *choice*, Sarah! If you'r
worrying about your reputation, don't bother. Fo
all they know, there are a dozen of us down her
You'll recall I neglected to tell them the camp i
deserted. Otherwise Tony might come chargin
down here to police his claim.'

She raised her voice against the hysterica
shriek of the wind. 'I don't need you to champio
my virtue, thank you!'

Guy snorted derisively. 'Look,' he said, sound
ing very close to exasperation, 'I'm just a
annoyed as you are at this hitch. But I sugges
that for tonight, at least, we forget personal ani
mosities and turn our attention to saving ou
necks!'

With the snowmobile tucked into the shelter c
the igloo, a tarpaulin roped securely over it, Gu
and Sarah struggled against the storm with thei
precious bundles of supplies. The blizzard wa

descending on them with terrifying speed. The
gloo, which had seemed within arm's reach only
moments before, now receded into the swirling
now.

Enclosed in a world of total whiteness, Sarah
tumbled blindly down some crude ice steps. Guy
yanked back the flap of skin that covered the en-
trance tunnel. Roughly, his hand found the top of
her head and pressed her to her knees. The wind
and thick snow vanished, but were replaced by a
silence and darkness that were equally disconcerting.

'I can't see!' she protested, inching haltingly
along the constricting tunnel.

'Just feel ahead of you!' he ordered from behind
her. 'It will open out in another foot or two.'

Cautiously she did as she was told, suppressing
a nibble of horror at the thought of what might
lie ahead in the blackness. She heard fumbling,
tinny noises and the striking of a match. A pale
orange flame flared and grew, bathing them in
golden light and casting tall, wildly flickering
shadows on the dome above them.

'What do you think?' said Guy, setting the lantern down on a wide, raised platform in front of
them.

Sarah pushed back her hood and brushed snow
from her bangs. 'It's bigger than I thought it
would be. And more intricate.'

'Igloos are nothing short of ingenious,' he said,
rummaging through a dunnage bag. 'Those ice

blocks actually form an inward spiral. And this
pit that we're in now traps the cold air and keeps
it away from the sleeping platform. A more permanent shelter would have glazed walls, ice
windows, carved storage areas, and . . . well, that's
a bonus!'

He pointed to a pile of animal skins lining the
sleeping area. 'They'll insulate us from below.'

Sarah regarded them unenthusiastically. She
said, suddenly very sober, 'Is there any chance—
really—that we could freeze here tonight? I want
you to tell me the truth. I promise I won't get
hysterical or cry.'

'None,' he replied firmly. 'And I'm not saying
that just to be easy on you. We'll be uncomfortable, we'll have to use common sense. But our
clothes and sleeping bags are designed for the
Arctic. We've got warm food, and each other.
Trust me.'

The temperature inside their shelter was plum-
meting rapidly and a bone-deep cold was beginning to seep through their clothes. Quickly they
finished unpacking their supplies. Sarah sat back
on her heels and regarded all that stood between
them and an icy death: two sleeping bags, a first
aid kit, tiny packets of freeze-dried food, a minute
solid fuel stove.

'Oh, Guy,' she said wistfully, 'just a few miles
back there lies warmth and clean sheets and the
Enterprise's cooks making lovely things for dinner!
It's such a short distance . . . we could even walk

it if it weren't for the storm.'

Guy was priming the stove, heating them sweet tea to keep up their resistance to the cold. 'I have something else that will cheer you up,' he said. 'Something not on the official list of survival supplies.' He dug into an inside picket and produced a silver flask. 'Good French brandy,' he announced. He poured some into the cap and handed it to her. 'Drink it,' he ordered. 'It'll do you good.'

Sarah sipped and felt the soft warmth spread through her. Revived a little, she propped one of the rolled sleeping bags against the wall and leaned back. What an odd place for the two of them to end up in! she thought, sipping more brandy. Trapped in that pale capsule of dancing amber light, half buried beneath drifting, obliterating snow.

What were the people back at the ship thinking now? Did they know it was like this? She stole a cautious look at Guy as he took a long drink from the flask. His chin was tipped, exposing the underside of his jaw and the pulse point there. Perhaps it was just the brandy, but she felt that suddenly a peace had fallen over them.

'It's funny, isn't it?' she said dreamily. 'Here we are, horrified at the thought of spending a single night in the north, even though people have survived under these conditions, without all our equipment, for hundreds of years.'

He leaned back beside her, long legs outstretched, his ankles crossed casually. 'You're right there. It's not the climate that poses the threat to the native culture.'

'I guess you mean the *Enterprise* does,' she replied. 'You know, since you're a part owner of Freeland Shipping, I find your hostility towards the ship incomprehensible. What do you hope to gain, undermining her the way you do?'

'Is that what you really think, or are you parroting things you hear Tony say?'

'I form my own opinions, Guy. And I'd have to be blind not to see your aversion.'

'Everything I do on the *Enterprise*, I do for the good of the entire company. I wish I could say the same for Tony. He couldn't wait to thrust Freeland Shipping into the twenty-first century, whether it was ready for it or not.'

The brandy was beginning to unleash Sarah from prudent restraint. 'Rumour has it,' she said, 'that you and Tony fought it out in the boardroom over the L.N.G. contract and that you lost.'

Even in that ghostly light, she could see anger flare his nostrils. 'There's some truth in that, I suppose,' he said, his voice dangerously calm. 'But I didn't oppose the *Enterprise* in principle . . . I was against certain terms of Tony's proposal that eventually won us the contract. I won't say what those terms were.'

Sarah felt piqued. 'I wasn't asking you to tell me any secrets,' she replied defensively.

'There's only one thing you need to know,' he

said. 'No matter what problems there may be between Tony and me, I don't let my personal feelings affect my professional judgment. Now that
the *Arctic Enterprise* is a reality, I only want her
to succeed.'

'Did it ever occur to you,' she asked, pulling
her knees tight to her chest and wrapping her
arms around them, 'that in trying to master your
job, you've become bogged down in detail and
lost your perspective?'

'I see . . . and it takes a mind like Tony's to
give purpose and direction to the company?'

'Those are your words, not mine!'

'Well, that's what would pass for a theory from
someone who hasn't the faintest idea what she's
talking about.'

'You have the most amazing ego I've ever had
the misfortune to be cooped up with!' she
snapped, flaring.

'That's tough,' he said unpleasantly. 'But I deal
in facts . . . in all those tiresome details that get in
the way of the soaring visionary minds like
Tony's. I also deal in the price others pay for the
gambles of their superiors. Tony's never pulled a
charred hunk of flesh that used to be a man out of
some blasted wreckage—I have.'

'And that's how you see the *Enterprise*. Just
another disaster waiting to happen?'

'God, I hope not, I really do.'

'Tell me something,' she prodded. 'Have you
seen a single thing on the *Enterprise* that gives

you grounds for your fears?'

'No,' he observed slowly. 'On the contrary, I'm impressed. Now, have you got what you were pushing for?'

'What is that supposed to mean?'

'It means that you probably feel quite justified, now, in writing a nice, cheery story that your readers can thumb through over their breakfast coffee. No difficult issues to wrestle with, nothing to cloud their day.'

So much for their truce! Sarah fumed silently. She tried, unsuccessfully, to push away the suspicion that had been nibbling at her for days, now—that Guy thought she had been brought aboard the *Enterprise* for the sole purpose of whitewashing the venture.

If that were true, then in his eyes she had to be one of two things: either a wide-eyed ingénue who had fallen at Tony's feet, dazzled by his wealth and social position ... or a scheming, grasping opportunist. Surely she was wrong. He couldn't believe that of her!

She had come to agree with so many of the things he said. She had learned to give him grudging respect. In other circumstances, she thought they might have been friends. But instead, the gap between them widened at lightning speed.

She looked at the chiselled profile, the cheekbones underlined by the leaping shadows. The ruddy glow of his cheeks had intensified, and the cleft in his chin deepened.

Like Tony, he had all the culture and refinement of his position. But unlike his cousin, who had honed and polished himself to perfection, Guy seemed carelessly unaware of his appeal. The life he'd lived had coarsened him just enough to make him interesting. It had made him a man of contrasts and contradictions. He had a brilliant mind, schooled in the most advanced technology, yet he championed the oldest, most traditional forms of seamanship.

The sensible thing to do was to confront him with her suspicions and defend herself. Yet her pride stood firmly in the way. She realised that she was hurt just to think that he might hold such a low opinion of her. She was hurt very badly.

Without warning, Sarah began to shiver uncontrollably. As she sat with her painful musing, the gale had borne down on them in earnest and the temperature had dropped past zero.

'Talk's over,' said Guy, springing to a crouch. 'It's going to be a long, bitter night. I'll organise the supplies in arm's reach, you zip those two bags together.'

'I will not. I'll sleep on my own, if you don't mind,' she said with as much dignity as she could muster.

'I do mind. You may want to freeze to death to protect your precious modesty, but I don't. You don't think I have designs on your body, do you?' he asked witheringly.

'Of course not,' she snapped, but she turned her back to him so that he could not see the blood that burned in her cheeks.

She yanked off her mittens and her fingers stiffened instantly from the shock of the cold. Clumsily, she struggled with the two zippers, her hands unfeeling, until she succeeded in forming a single plump bag.

They removed their heavy boots and stuffed their parkas down inside the sleeping bag. 'But leave your cap on,' Guy warned. 'You lose a lot of heat through your head.'

Ill at ease, her teeth chattering, Sarah climbed into the bag, followed roughly by Guy. He reached out and turned off the lantern, plunging them into a blackness so total that Sarah had to resist the impulse to cry out against it.

She was now more worried about their fate than she cared to admit to him. The cold was truly terrifying. Her feet and hands ached so badly she could have cried. Her whole body cried out for warmth and sleep.

She felt Guy roll to his side and cup himself to her, his thighs snug behind hers, her bottom resting in the bend of his hips. She wished she did not crave the warm enclosure of his body, but she did—desperately. The cocoon of heat he formed around her was irresistible. Slowly, slowly her anger-tensed muscles relaxed and she uncoiled gratefully against his sheltering body.

As the long Arctic night closed around them,

she heard his breathing deepen, gradually taking on the rhythm of sleep. His breath was gentle against her neck. He was asleep, and she was, she supposed, safe. He had absolutely no intention of taking advantage of their situation, despite the kiss he had once wrenched from her.

Behind her, he stirred and murmured something unintelligible. His arm slipped around her waist and loosely cupped her breast. She held her breath, but he did not wake.

Pressing her eyelids tightly together, she willed sleep to come for her, too. But it evaded her, held at bay by the irresistible pleasure that had begun to flow through her. Desire stirred in her for a man who slept, uncaring, beside her. For the first time in her life she felt the pain of a wanting that was not returned. The extent of her need for Guy shocked her.

Only much later did exhaustion push her down into a restless, dream-filled sleep as troubled as the night around them. In her nightmares she saw herself imprisoned in a floating, suffocating bubble, drifting away from everything she knew, being sucked into a swirling, icy vortex. She called out his name in anguish.

Groggy with sleep, Guy turned on to his back, his strong arm dragging her half on top of him. Her head came to rest in the hollow of his shoulder, her leg between his thighs. Her eyes opened, and the dream vanished. But the cold had not gone away. Shivering, she burrowed into his

embrace like a tiny, soft animal. Though still
asleep, he responded to her soft, demanding presence. He brought a hand to her cheek and pressed
her face gently to his.

His lips were still soft with sleep against her
temple. She knew that for this one frozen moment
in time, there would be no hard, accusing words
from that mouth. A dreamlike longing washed
over her.

For so long she had postponed love. There had
been too many men who had not seemed worth
the distraction from her goals. Men who gave her
moments of gentle pleasure, but who never intrigued, maddened and, ultimately, inflamed her
the way this man now did.

She gave herself over to the sweet delight of
feeling him. Her fingers traced the planes of his
face and the crinkles at the corners of his eyes
that she had come to know so well. His power
and strength drew her like a magnet. Here was a
man that complemented her in will.

The defences that she had marshalled so carefully over the years began to fall away. She no
longer wanted to argue or find fault—or deny her
yearning one moment longer. She wanted him to
make love to her.

'. . . Sarah?' He was awake now, concern for
her in his hoarse voice.

'I'm here . . .' she whispered. 'It's all right . . .'

He spoke her name again, his voice low and
insistent. In answer, she tilted her chin, brushing

her lips against his with exquisite tenderness.

His mouth closed over hers, tentatively at first. But when he heard the tiny, sobbing breath she drew and understood her need of him, he unleashed the full power of his passion. His lips parted hers, drawing soft moans from her.

He took her hips easily in his large hands and in a smooth, forceful movement, shifted her off of him and pressed her back on to the voluptuous layers of down and fur. The weight of his body obliterated whatever reserve she had left. In reply to his hypnotic movement she lifted her hips to him, her arms circling his neck, her face buried in helpless surrender against his chest.

Crouched over her, his knees pinning her beneath him, Guy slipped his hands beneath her sweater, pulling it up to expose the curve of her tiny waist. Like a worshipper, he kissed her tenderly from side to side, then drew his tongue lightly from her navel to the bottom curve of her breast.

Sarah's head arched to one side. 'Oh, Guy . . . Guy!'

His hands slid up to her shoulders and he pressed his forehead against her stomach. 'I know . . . I know,' he whispered. He was struggling for his voice, and she understood that he, too, was experiencing a pleasure so intense that it verged on agony. Lowering himself on to her again, he cupped her face in his hands and covered it with a dozen longing kisses.

'You're so beautiful,' he murmured, his voice rough with passion. 'I've wanted you—you knew that!'

She hadn't. Not really. But the knowledge that he did stripped her emotions bare. She clung to him like a woman drowning, for no one, ever, had loosed such feeling in her.

'Trust me,' he whispered, cradling and stroking her. 'I want this to be so good for you, better than it ever was with Tony. You're going to forget him, Sarah.'

It was like a fist in her stomach. She felt choked with the nausea that rose in her. The heat that had flushed her skin seconds before was replaced by a chill that left her clammy and shivering. Wounded, yet outraged, she tried to scramble out of his embrace.

'Better than *what* with Tony!' she demanded in a strangled voice. 'You think I *sleep* with him, don't you!'

Startled by the intensity of her reaction, Guy pulled back from her. 'Don't try to tell me,' he scoffed, 'that you're going to plead innocence— not after the display of expertise I've just witnessed! I've seen the two of you together. I heard you accept his invitation to stay with him in England. In fact, you made very sure we all heard you, didn't you?'

'No!' she pleaded. 'It's not that way at all—you don't understand!'

'Oh, come on, Sarah!' he taunted. 'Everyone

knows what an aphrodisiac wealth and power is. Why should you be any more immune to it than other women?'

The brutal cutting off of pleasure was a physical pain. And so was the understanding that her first true response to sensuality, given so lovingly and unashamedly, had been perceived as the soulless performance of a seasoned professional. What she had offered him so ingenuously was being tossed back at her with an experienced man's scorn and disrespect.

At least the darkness hid her tears from him. 'I loathe you,' she said. 'I think I've hated you and your insufferable ego since I first saw you!'

'Maybe you do,' he jeered. 'But that didn't stop me from exciting you.'

'You *don't* excite me!' she shot back, knowing even as she spoke how ridiculous her protest must have sounded. Fluttering in his arms like a bird snared in a net, she pushed him away and huddled miserably as far from him as the narrow confines of the sleeping bag would allow.

The Arctic sun rose clear and bright, igniting a billion sparks in the unsullied snow that blanketed the land. Crawling on hands and knees from the mouth of the tunnel, Sarah blinked in pain at the brilliance of the morning.

She stood still for a very long time, staring at the glory of the untouched snow, and marvelled that they had survived the night. At least, physically, they had come through. But in no other way had she and Guy survived, she knew with a bitter, aching heart. Whatever relationship they had once struggled to maintain was now shattered, completely and for ever. The radiance of the dawn held only mockery for her.

CHAPTER SEVEN

'TERRIFIED!' pronounced Katie. 'I'd be quaking in my boots. But having a man like Captain Court to look after you must have been a comfort.'

'Uh-huh ...' murmured Sarah noncommittally.

'I'll bet he took right over,' Katie breezed on. 'And what about the hunters at the camp? You haven't told us anything——'

'Look!' cried Sarah, relief flooding her voice. 'Here's Mr Dunn. Perhaps he can tell us what's happening.'

Ever since the two young women had met in the lounge that afternoon, Katie had been trying to extract information from Sarah about the three-hour excursion that had turned into an overnight drama. Sarah had dodged and weaved as best she could, but she was fast running out of stories about the joys of spotting a snow goose or a seal sunning itself.

'This is a far cry from the water we came in through, Mr Dunn,' she said, raising binoculars to her eyes and sweeping the vast ice field.

'Yes, indeed,' agreed Angus, wiping greasy hands on well-used coveralls. 'That delay at Melville put us square into winter and no mistake about it! We're breaking ice up to five feet in places.'

Sarah listened with relief to the chatter about the heavy weather that had dogged them since they left the island. She wanted desperately to distract herself from memories of Guy's abortive and humiliating lovemaking. Yet just a single flash of remembrance of his touch on her skin held the power to enflame her. With an exercise of will that stretched taut the sinews of her neck, she dragged her attention back to her companions.

'But the ice—that's no problem, is it?' she asked with forced interest.

'Oh, no,' the First Engineer replied, smiling. 'We're built for worse than this!'

Their first day out, the bands of ice on either side of the strait had thickened rapidly, narrowing the water lane until at last the *Enterprise* had struck solid resistence. Low, dense ice fog had begun to plague them. The cold was never less than cruel for any of the crew unlucky enough to draw outside duty under the coarse woollen clouds.

And there was also the new, silent presence on the *Enterprise* that affected the crew's spirits far more than the weather: the millions of gallons of super-cold liquid gas that now lay beneath them. But at least those nerve-jangling, unpredictable alarm bells signalling another of Guy's drills were silent for this leg of the journey. Still, he remained a constant observer, forever moving, monitoring,

ARCTIC ENEMY   135

observing every procedure. Tony, in contrast, was
surprisingly relaxed now that the snag at the
pumping station was behind them. He was looking forward with relish to a triumphant arrival in
Nova Scotia, with welcoming ceremonies and
television coverage.

Sarah wished she could share Tony's elation,
but her thoughts kept returning to their volatile
cargo and the battering it was receiving. Time
after time, the *Enterprise*'s bow drove up on to the
ice pack. There was a pause, then the ice fractured
and gave way under the tremendous weight of the
steel-banded hull. Released, the ship fell seaward,
having carved a little more of its tortuous path.

By late afternoon when Sarah reached Tony's
suite for a pre-dinner drink, the constant heaving
of the decks had begun to affect her stomach.

'I think,' she told him as he greeted her, 'that
I'd better sit down . . . quickly!'

Tony smiled down on her sympathetically.
'We'll be clearing the ice any time now. Just hold
on a little longer.'

'I'll try,' she replied, laying a hand gingerly on
her stomach. 'But I don't know if I can handle
that drink, Tony.'

'Nonsense. It'll relax you. You've been tense
ever since you returned from that ill-advised excursion with my adventuresome cousin. Really,
Sarah, every time I think about that I get so angry
I could——'

'Tony, please. It was no one's fault . . . except,

perhaps, mine. I was the one who made such a big fuss about seeing something of the island before we left. Anyway, no harm was done, and I did get some good atmosphere material for the story. I expect I'm just feeling the pressure of the deadline coming up.'

Tony looked at her solicitously and picked up the tiny porcelain hand that lay across her knee. He had touched her hand before, of course. But this time Sarah could feel a difference. His grasp was more insistent, almost possessive.

Perversely, Tony's touch brought an unwelcome picture of Guy to her mind's eye. She gave a slight shake of her swinging auburn hair as if to rid herself of his spectre. Impulsively, as if she could somehow punish Guy, she returned the pressure of Tony's hand.

'I've neglected you these last few days,' he said. 'But I'm going to make up for that when you join me in England. You haven't forgotten your promise?'

'No,' she said, with a sad, twisted smile. She looked up at him and realised that he was going to kiss her. Her reaction was curiously cold-blooded, as if she was the dispassionate observer of an experiment. Would she respond to him as she had to Guy?

She watched his gently parted lips move slowly towards her, then closed her eyes and accepted him in a robot-like reply. Encouraged by her passiveness, he became more demanding until she was finally jolted out of her numbness and murmured a small protest.

'All right, my darling, I won't press you. Just let me hold you for a moment—please.' He eased his pressure on her but did not release her entirely. He laid his cheek on top of her head and stroked her hair soothingly.

How could she rebuff him? He was ardent, yet so gentle. He accepted her silence as consent and continued to hold her head against his shoulder, not suspecting what sadness and conflict lay at the core of her muteness.

What am I doing? she thought, confusion knitting her brow. Any normal woman would be flattered by the attentions of Tony Freeland. He was all the things that Katie had so enthusiastically enumerated, and offered to open the door for her to a delightful interlude in her life.

Yet she was so curiously unmoved. Why did she feel so frozen, so cut off from her emotions and her body? Guy had no trouble in making her respond to his blatant, aggressive advances. The memory of them made her cheeks flame. She twisted her face into Tony's suit jacket so that he wouldn't see the colour that spread down her neck and think it came for him.

Her brusied ego craved the balm of Tony's affection. Yet she felt such a fraud in his arms! It was selfish and deceitful, and she hated it.

Tony's glass slid the length of the coffee table and crashed into Sarah's, splashing sherry over the hem of her skirt.

'Oh, Sarah, I'm sorry,' he began.

'It's all right,' she said quickly, guilty at the relief she felt in being free of his arms. 'I'll get a napkin.'

As she stood, the roll of the ship sent her staggering, and only Tony's lunge for her kept her on her feet. The two stood clinging to each other, struggling for footing as the *Enterprise* righted herself and began a rolling pitch to the opposite side.

'Tony, look out there!' Sarah cried, pointing to the windows.

They had broken free of the ice-bound straits into the waters of Baffin Bay. The open sea was horrifyingly vast and green and cold. The sky was an ugly, mottled purple. Huge ice floes swirled slowly in the Greenland current, hinting darkly at their hidden power to grind and destroy. Immense swells surged against the hull, shooting high before raining down on the deck.

'A little humbling, wouldn't you say?' asked Sarah, hugging herself as a shiver travelled the length of her spine.

'You're not frightened, are you?' Tony laid both hands on her shoulders and twisted her to face him. 'Look, if it will help banish your fears, why don't we visit the bridge? We can hear the latest weather report, and you'll be able to see for yourself that the officers don't give a blow like this a second thought.'

Sarah stopped short as they entered the unusually crowded bridge and met Guy's hostile glare head-on. Squaring her neat shoulders and tossing her head back slightly, she held firm to Tony's arm with a proprietorial air that he could not miss. She knew it was a transparent, almost childish ploy, but she delighted shamelessly in its obvious success, noting the way Guy's eyes flashed as he watched them cross the room.

Patrick looked harassed, with smudges of weariness underlining his eyes. He didn't seem particularly pleased to see his employer, Sarah thought, but managed a perfunctory smile.

'The winds are almost up to gale force, Mr Freeland,' he replied to Tony's question, 'with no signs of slackening.' Then, seeing the alarm on Sarah's face, he added quickly, 'But we'll weather it, of course. If it gets to you, Sarah, you can get something from the medical officer to settle your stomach.'

'Thank you, Patrick. I may do that.'

He smiled ruefully. 'Poor Katie's taken to her bed with nausea. Keep your flat shoes on, and try to remember to keep your knees loose and flexible to absorb the pitching of the deck.'

'I do try,' said Sarah, frowning, 'but I can't quite get the hang of the rolling sailor's gait that——'

An angry voice rose over the general hum of machinery. Sarah peeped over Patrick's shoulder and saw two red-faced junior officers confronting each other, tempers snapping.

'What's the problem, Benton?' Patrick demanded.

'That last course change you ordered to avoid that berg, sir. It wasn't executed properly,' he replied tensely.

'Well, Stuart?' asked Patrick of the other man.

'The helmsman looked stiff but defiant. 'I executed the change as ordered, sir. I was just about to show Benton the record.'

Patrick looked at the book, then turned questioningly to Benton. 'Everything looks in order . . .'

'But it's not, sir,' he protested. 'Our position doesn't jibe.'

'Do your calculations again,' Patrick instructed.

He did, and the same infuriating discrepancy appeared.

'Take a manual fix, Patrick.' It was Guy. He'd been following the tense exchange and now appeared from the shadows at the back of the bridge.

'Yes, of course,' said Patrick, his eyes expressing gratitude for the calming, sensible suggestion.

A sighting was taken on the stars using the same techniques known to sailors for hundreds of years. The tried-and-true method revealed that although the wheel had been put ten degrees to port, the bow had actually moved that way only marginally. The crew was stunned into silence by the implications of that news.

'It's the steering,' said Patrick at last, his voice betraying disbelief. 'It's not responding properly.' Jolted into action, he dispatched a cadet to summon the master and sent out an urgent call for Angus Dunn as well.

Captain Price appeared within minutes, still buttoning his shirt. He assessed the situation rapidly. After ordering a radical course alteration to compensate for the unresponsiveness of the steering, he sent Angus and two technicians down to the steering control room to try to find the cause of the malfunction.

'The weather?' he asked Patrick, his manner still utterly calm.

'Winds are sixty miles per hour with no moderation, sir. Gale force expected by nightfall—possibly as high as a hundred.'

'And ice?'

'Radar shows several large bergs bearing down on us. One is passing us now close to the starboard side.'

'Too close, Patrick.'

'Yes, sir.'

'Why in heaven's name are they creating this melodrama!' whispered Tony harshly. 'This ship was designed to withstand the worst ice conditions.'

'There's a hell of a difference between an ice-field and an iceberg,' said Guy impatiently.

'Don't lecture me!' Tony snapped furiously.

'Please!' hissed Sarah, her eyes darting frantically to the crew. There was always just enough truth or logic in everything Guy said to make it difficult to argue with him and win—as she had discovered to her own chagrin. But the nagging suspicion that there was substance to everything he said only seemed to stiffen her against him.

'We'll have to make a substantial cut in speed, Patrick.' The Master's voice was disturbingly grave. 'Order a change to——'

Tony's voice slashed across his. 'There'll be no slowing down, Captain!'

Captain Price swivelled slowly around in his raised chair and looked quizzically at him. Every man on the bridge was silent, shock plainly written across his face.

'Perhaps you don't understand our situation, Mr Freeland,' he replied steadily. 'We're in very heavy seas. Our L.N.G. load is beginning to give us a roll effect, and our steering is not as precise as it should be. No prudent Master would continue to move through seas like these at full speed. Now, Mr Freeland—my ship needs my full attention.'

But Tony was in no mood to be put off. 'We're three days behind schedule and you tell me you want to be "prudent"! Well, I don't pay you top salary to have you run this ship like some nervous cadet. You're supposed to have the brains and experience to handle a situation like this!'

Dear lord, Tony! thought Sarah. How can you speak to him like that? She could barely believe her ears.

Captain Price was unshakably polite. 'I repeat: only a fool would push a ship through waves like those. She's too big, Mr Freeland. She can't ride them like conventional tankers. If she gets hung up on the crest of a giant wave with her bow and her stern hanging over the troughs, the weight of the L.N.G. could snap her back. It would be the end of us.'

'And are the seas that bad yet?'

'No . . . not yet. But may I remind you that the *Enterprise* is untried in gale conditions?' He turned away from Tony. 'Helmsman—half speed!'

'No!' shouted Tony, striding over to the bewildered crewman, who stood with his hand hovering above the controls. The proverbial pin could have been heard dropping.

The Master's voice rang out, clear and authoritative. 'This ship's charter names me her Master, under God. *Under God*, Mr Freeland! Next to the good Lord himself, I have the sole responsibility for this ship and every life on board her. And with that authority, I will order you off the bridge and into your quarters, under guard, if necessary, if you attempt again to interfere with my command. Is that quite clear, sir?'

A dark shadow passed over Tony's eyes. His fists clenched and unclenched. 'All right, Price . . . for now. But you'll never command the

Enterprise again. Nor any other ship. I'll see to it.' He spun on his heel and strode out of the bridge, leaving the door banging wildly on its hinges.

As a cadet scurried to close the door, Sarah exhaled painfully. She had been holding her breath during the exchange until her chest ached. It had been an ugly piece of business, and it had shaken her profoundly. She looked up and saw Guy's eyes boring into her.

'Don't say it,' she blurted out. 'Just don't— say—a thing!'

'Why do you think I'm going to say something?' he asked sardonically.

'Because I'm beginning to understand you. Because I know you always have some sarcastic, taunting comment at the tip of your tongue. Well, I won't let you put me in the position of defending Tony!'

'Then you admit he needs defending?'

'I admit nothing,' she snapped. 'Tony's within his rights to question the running of the *Enterprise*. He'd be remiss if he didn't.'

There—he'd done it again! Had her standing up for Tony. Or had she done it to herself? She'd seen nothing to admire in Tony's treatment of Captain Price, either. He'd displayed a side of himself she hadn't known existed. But her need to protect her bruised pride kept her from admitting that to Guy.

Hurrying steps rang out on the inner staircase

and Angus Dunn appeared, black with oil and
glistening with sweat.

'Luck, Angus?' asked the Master sharply.

'If you want to call it that.' he replied wearily,
mopping his brow with a stained rag. 'It's only a
guess, sir, but I figure that those waves out there
put terrific pressure on the rudder. That pressure
was transmitted back through the hydraulic
lines—we found a couple of key bolts sheared
right off by it!'

'Can you fix it?' asked Patrick.

'We've already jury-rigged something. You
should have control back now.'

Orders were given at once to the helmsman,
who performed a series of manoeuvres. The navigation officer double-checked their position and
confirmed that the steering mechanism was working again.

'But I don't mind telling you, Captain,' said
Angus, 'I don't like it a bit. We're rolling heavily
and it's going to get worse before we see daylight.
If we blow another fitting, I can't promise I'll
have as much luck a second time. It's murder
down in the gear compartment—there's oil every-
where. I've already sent two of my men to sick
bay with cuts from the falls they've taken.'

Captain Price drummed his fingers on the arm
of his chair. 'We'll order extra watches, keep our
speed as low as we can without losing control . . .
and pray that this thing blows itself out soon.
Patrick, order every man not on essential duty to

get all the sleep he can. Heaven knows when any
of *us* will see our beds again.'

As Angus turned to leave, Guy pulled him to
one side. 'Those bolts that broke off the hydraulic
line—could I see them?'

Angus peered at him, his eyes narrowing. 'Sure,
Guy. I'll send a man up with them right away.'

Minutes later, a cadet flew up the stairs and
presented Guy with a greasy box. Sarah watched
as he set it on the chart table and swivelled a light
on to it. Frowning, he turned the bolts over and
over in his hands. Then, throwing them back into
the box, he switched off the light and let himself
out on to the flying bridge.

Curious, Sarah went to the table and looked
into the box. The bolts were oversized, like
everything else on the *Enterprise*, and they had
sharp, smooth planes where they had snapped off
their fittings. Otherwise they looked perfectly
ordinary. She couldn't imagine what had riveted
Guy's attention for so long. She grabbed her
parka from its hook and zipped it hastily.

She found him at the rail, staring out at the
storm, his long legs spread wide against the buck-
ing deck. Even in that punishing wind, she
thought, he looked powerful and in control.

She lurched towards him, her hands gripping
her hood. 'Guy!' she shouted, and he turned,
reached out, and dragged her the last few feet to
the rail.

'What are you doing out here? Are you insane?'

'I want to know what's really going on! I don't
care bother anyone in there. Is that repair of
Angus's going to hold?'

'What can I say to you, Sarah—we'll just have
o pray that it will.'

'But I heard one of the men talking about
ounding the alarm for lifeboat stations!'

He shook his head vehemently. 'He was only
eviewing what the rule book tells him he should
e doing in a situation like this. We're still a long
vay from having to face that decision. Anyway, it
vould be a desperation move. Even if we could
et the boats away in time, our chances of surviv-
ng in the sea are infinitesimal.'

Sarah looked out over the boiling sea. Yes, she
hought. Infinitesimal. For a moment she could
aste a bitter knot of fear hardening in her
hroat.

Guy watched her coldly as she absorbed the
eriousness of their situation. 'No, it wouldn't be
 very nice end.' he said, reading her thoughts.
What an anticlimax for Tony's glorious adven-
ure!'

'Why must you always assign blame? Tony
idn't cause this storm!'

'And why must you always defend him? No,
orget that I asked. I'm sick to death of the merry-
o-round you and I are on. I couldn't care less
bout what you do or why you do it. I used to
vonder, but it hardly seems important at a time
ike this.'

Tears of frustration sprang to Sarah's eyes. . had all turned out so badly. She hadn't wanted to be like this between them.

He bent down to her, shouting against th wind's howl. 'She's a great ship, and she'll get u through this! You remember that. Now, go belov Stay in your cabin—we don't need you wanderin about and getting a leg broken. And keep your lif preserver by the door, just in case. Do you rememb your lifeboat station?'

She nodded, pulling back the veil of hair th had whipped across her face.

'Go on,' he said, pushing her towards the doo 'That's an order!'

She didn't delude herself that his concern fo her safety sprang from any feeling for her. N Guy Court would do as much for anyone. It wa simply his duty. As she turned to yank the doo shut after her, she took one last look at the wave that loomed like walls above them. Yes, sh thought, it had come true. The *Arctic Enterpri.* really was standing into danger.

CHAPTER EIGHT

DUTIFULLY, as if by acting sanely she could impose order on a situation that seemed to be rushing headlong out of control, Sarah had gone to her cabin. The steward was cheerful and solicitous, leaving words of reassurance along with a tray of sandwiches and hot chocolate, but she was unable to eat.

The dishes did a shuddering dance across the table, jangling her already raw nerves. The deep lunges of the ship, combined with the thrumming vibration of the giant screws made her head throb unbearably and her vision blur. She tottered to the washroom and swallowed the pills the medical officer had delivered. They took the edge off the pain and nausea, but did little to ease her concern.

She slept, but only briefly. A titanic wave jolted the *Enterprise*, tossing her almost off her bunk. She struggled upright, rubbing the shoulder that stung painfully from its collision with the bedside table. She switched on the wall light. Four a.m. It was still coal black outside her porthole. Sleep was out, and so was writing.

Cautiously, she padded barefoot to the washroom and splashed cold water on her face. Perhaps

if she looked bright and confident, she might fe
it, she reasoned. Defiantly she applied make-u
and brushed her hair back into the shinin
swinging perfection that was her trademark. I
her best cable knit pullover and pants, she wende
her way up to the bridge.

They were all there—still. There had been
change in the secondary crew, but Captain Pric
Patrick, and Guy stood watch as before, exhaus
tion ringing their eyes. Guy saw her, showe
momentary surprise, then turned his attentio
wordlessly back to his work. But just that sing
flashing glance was enough to make her giddy.

Patrick sat slumped over a pile of charts, crad
ing one of the many mugs of coffee that ha
brought him through the night. His smile was wa
but welcoming, and Sarah joined him.

'Excuse me for saying this, Patrick,' she sai
perching on the stool across from him, 'but yc
look dreadful. Didn't you get *any* rest?'

'No,' he laughed, rubbing his palms weari
over his face. 'But that comes with the territor
I'm afraid.'

'There's not much change in the weather,
there?' she noted, looking at the spray-lashe
windows. Dawn was beginning to break, stainir
the horizon a malevolent blood red more sugges
ive of hell than a new day.

She rested her chin on one hand and sighed.
wish I could be braver, but frankly, I'm scare
silly.'

Patrick grinned and patted her hand. 'Well, you don't *look* scared silly. In fact, I'll wager you've delighted every bleary pair of eyes on the bridge.'

Not every pair, thought Sarah, glancing at Guy's broad back. 'How's the steering holding up?' she asked, dragging her eyes off him.

Patrick shrugged. 'So far, so good. If we can just hang on another hour ... two at the most, I think we'll be home free.'

The outside door slid open, admitting the screaming fury of the wind. A lookout, in oilskins stiff with frozen spray, lurched in, binoculars swinging from his neck. He headed straight for the Captain.

'We picked it up when the light started to break, sir,' she heard him say. 'We're getting wave damage to one of the valve covers near the bow.'

'Are you absolutely certain?'

'As much as we can be. One of the covers seems to be hanging askew, but I couldn't send a man out there for a closer look—it would be sure death, sir.'

'Yes ... yes,' the Master agreed, rubbing his hand wearily over his brow. The crew exchanged appalled looks over this latest blow.

When the Master finally spoke, his voice was very quiet. 'This is a bad business, men. If that cover goes and the valve is exposed to these waves, I don't have to tell you what it could mean. And in our present circumstances, I don't see how we can effect repairs.'

'But those covers shouldn't go!' Guy said firmly; his fist slamming down on the rail. ' designed them to withstand anything so that th valves would never go unprotected!'

Sarah watched, eyes wide, as he detached him self abruptly from the huddle of officers and strode over to the chart table. Was *he* responsibl for this latest calamity? 'If you need me,' he said grimly to Patrick, 'I'll be in Tony's suite.'

Sarah leaned across the table and placed a hand urgently on Patrick's arm. 'What's all *this* about she demanded.

Patrick hesitated, as if assessing her. Then, 'O L.N.G. tankers, there's an awful lot of pipin exposed on the deck. Crucial things, like the tan valves, are under protective shields. Apparentl one of them is giving way under all the wate that's crashing down on the decks. If it goe before the storm lets up, then it's conceivable tha some of the L.N.G. might escape.' He broke of and his eyes were suddenly far away, as if imagin ing the unthinkable.

'We could break up, then,' said Sarah simply.

Patrick started, and brought his attention bac to her. 'Oh, look, Sarah—that's the worst tha could happen. It's a one-in-a-million possibility The gale is peaking right now, and in an hour c so it'll be like a millpond out there.' He winke playfully at her as he stood to join the other mer but Sarah was not deceived. He was worried.

She slipped down off the stool and went to th

sideboard, where she poured herself some coffee.
She had missed two meals, and decided she
should at least make a stab at keeping up her
strength. She selected a warm biscuit from the
fare the steward had provided and wandered to
the windows.

Far ahead, the bows were now visible in the
cold grey light. She could understand why there
was no hope of a repair crew venturing out there.
As the *Enterprise* punched through the swells,
unable to ride on top of them the way a smaller
ship would, walls of water were being driven relentlessly down the length of the deck. The tons of
water that could buckle steel and wrench open
welds would surely crush bones and flesh.

It was a chastening sight, and Sarah turned her
back on it. Cupping her mug under her chin and
inhaling the reassuring aroma, she leaned back
against the rail and listened to the officers.

'We *have* to try,' one of them said. 'I just don't
see that we have any choice.'

The Captain turned his eyes questioningly to
his First Engineer. 'He has a point,' agreed Angus
reluctantly, 'but I still say you'd be throwing lives
away for nothing. None of my men could sort
through that maze fast enough in that whirlwind.
I say we gamble that it holds!'

'Who have you got who really knows that
equipment?'

The men looked at each other. 'Guy,' said
Angus. 'No question about it.'

'Where is he?' the Captain demanded, his keen dark eyes raking the room.

'With Mr Freeland, sir,' answered Patrick.

'What's he doing there—get him up here, man!' he snapped, for the first time displaying the effects of unrelenting pressure and hours without sleep.

Patrick went to the phone and dialled the state room, drumming his fingers impatiently. 'Come on . . . come on . . .' he muttered under his breath 'Why don't they answer!' he snapped at last, slamming down the receiver.

Sarah spoke up without hesitation. 'Let me go and get him. Then you won't have to take anyone away from his duty . . . please, Patrick, I feel so useless!'

'All right, Sarah—and tell him to hurry!'

A knock on the broad double door brought no reply. She pressed her ear to it, positive she had heard muffled voices. When a second, louder knock still brought no one, she opened the door and stuck her head in. The sitting room was empty, but beyond it, the door to Tony's bedroom stood open and the sound of raised, angry voices was clear.

Alarmed, Sarah let herself in, her footsteps silent on the thick broadloom.

'This is no coincidence—if you know something, Tony, you *must* tell me!' Guy's voice was tight with barely controlled anger.

'You're out of your mind,' Tony scoffed. '

haven't the slightest idea what you're ranting about.'

'Those bolts that sheared off the steering mechanism, and now the valve cover: I'd stake my life that the steel in them is less than the tensile strength my design specs called for!'

'Nothing on this ship is substandard. Every single piece of equipment on it meets the minimum legal requirements!' Tony shot back.

'For ordinary ships, maybe. But the *Enterprise*'s not an ordinary tanker, and she doesn't sail through ordinary waters. There was a reason for every safety standard I set for her. Look out of the window, for God's sake! Can't you see with your own eyes why I didn't want her compromised in any way?'

Sarah stood rooted to her spot, unable to move forward and make her presence known, and equally unable to retreat. I can't be hearing this! she thought, her heart thudding painfully. Did Guy realise what he was accusing his cousin of?

'No one could fathom how we were able to get this contract. How we were able to bid so low for such high quality. What else did you have the builder cut costs on, Tony?' Guy's voice cut across the air like a whip.

For the first time, Tony's icy control showed signs of slipping. 'I'm only going to say this once more, Guy. I ordered everything exactly as you engineers specified. I have no knowledge of any discrepancies!' His voice had risen and a thin note

of desperation had crept into it. But at the sam
time there was something flatly honest about it.

'No . . .' said Guy slowly, 'you probably don't
You didn't want to dirty your hands, did you
There's nothing on paper, nothing that I'll be abl
to trace back to you and your bloody greed an
ego. How did you do it, Tony? A glance . . .
sentence left unfinished . . . a "gentlemen's agree
ment" over brandy in your town house?'

'You'll never prove a thing,' Tony spat out
'Everything I've done is perfectly legal. You'v
lost, Guy. Face it! When we get back to London
when the *Enterprise* is acclaimed the success it'
going to be, you'll no longer be Uncle Julian's fair
haired boy! The company will be in the hands of on
strong leader, the way it was years ago and ought t
be now. I'm going to see to it that you won't even ge
a job on a tramp steamer after this!'

There was a crash and Sarah was galvanise
into action. She lunged for the bedroom door an
found them sprawled across the bed, Guy's hand
gripping Tony's collar, Tony's knee knifed int
the other's groin.

'Stop it—for heaven's sake, stop it!' sh
shrieked, pulling futilely at Guy's sweater. 'D
you want me to get the stewards?'

The two men stared at her, stunned by he
sudden appearance. She seized advantage of thei
momentary distraction. 'Captain Price wants yo
on the bridge immediately, Guy. It's an emer
gency—hurry!'

He took a last, contempt-filled look at Tony, then shook him off like something foul. Raking his hair back off his brow, he strode from the room.

Tony watched him disappear, his eyes narrow with loathing, and dabbed at the blood oozing from the corner of his mouth. 'How long have you been standing there?' he demanded, his chest rising and falling from exertion.

'Long enough to hear some very ugly charges,' Sarah retorted, her jaw tight.

He tossed his stained handkerchief on the bed and took her slender shoulders in his hands. 'My poor Sarah,' he said. 'I'm so sorry you had to see that. Guy's become completely unhinged, making those wild accusations. His own design errors have put us into this mess, and the man's casting about for someone else to blame.'

'Really?' said Sarah coldly. 'It didn't sound that way to me.'

'Don't you see, darling? He was in way over his head when he designed the *Enterprise*. Now he can't bear to face up to his own incompetence.'

Sarah stood very still, staring at the man whom she had so recently defended. 'I'll make it all up to you, I promise,' said Tony, fawning over her. 'As soon as we're together in England, we'll put all this behind us and things will be perfect again.'

'I was part of it, wasn't I?' she said in wonder. 'Sympathetic press coverage was something you needed badly if your scheme was going to work. I was the mindless little twit who would be so overwhelmed by all this wealth and dazzle that I'd write the most glowing story . . . why, it would be positively worshipful! And just to make sure I'd help set you up as some kind of hero, you decided to dangle all sorts of rewards in front of me. The poor, provincial girl who would be beside herself with joy at being noticed by the glamorous Anthony Freeland!'

She saw the shift in his eyes and knew she had hit the mark. 'Sarah, that's absurd. You're becoming hysterical!' He reached out to touch her cheek, but she slapped his hand away.

'Oh, no, Tony . . . quite the opposite. For the first time in days I'm seeing our situation very clearly. But the thing is, Tony, that it wouldn't have worked. Even if I had fallen in love with you—which I didn't, by the way—I would never have written the story you wanted me to. Because whatever else I may be, I'm honest. Your mistake was in thinking I was more woman than journalist. Unfortunately for you, the two aren't mutually exclusive.'

A sullen anger began to play about his mouth. 'Guy's got to you, I see,' he said stiffly.

'Guy . . . that's why he was so hostile to me, isn't it?' she said, understanding suddenly lifting her voice. 'He saw through your plan from the start and thought I was your accomplice, either through design or ignorance. Either way, he couldn't help but feel contempt for me.'

The mask of affection and concern fell completely from Tony's face. 'You can think what you will,' he jeered. 'But can you write such drivel? It's sheer supposition. And a very unattractive picture of you, I might add: an ambitious reporter, struck silly by a once-in-a-lifetime opportunity, throws herself at a wealthy man. When she's put in her place, she writes a false and malicious story in revenge.'

'That's not true!' she seethed.

'Isn't it? It's your word against mine, my dear, and I doubt very seriously whether anyone would believe you. Think about it for a moment, Sarah. You haven't got a single fact to back up any of your ravings. There's a word for that, Sarah—slander.' He jabbed a finger warningly in her face. 'If you print a word about these theories of Guy's—or these fantasies of yours about me trying to seduce you—my lawyers will break both you and your newspaper.'

They faced each other, anger snapping like an electric current between them. The harsh jangle of an alarm cracked the silence. 'Now what!' barked Tony, his eyes darting about the room in panic.

'It's the lifeboat call,' said Sarah, her voice a strangled whisper.

He burst past her, almost knocking her off her feet. He jerked open a closet door, pulled out a coat and lifejacket, and fled without a glance at her.

'Well,' she said, following after him, 'so much for the beautiful manners of the well-bred Mr Freeland!'

Stiff and awkward in their life jackets, Katie, Emily and Sarah huddled in the shelter of a stairway, beneath a fringe of dagger-sharp icicles. The officer in charge of their group had done his best to reassure them that the alarm was only a precaution, but they all sensed that the crisis had reached a critical point.

Katie's eyes were bright with unshed tears, her voice wistful. 'I haven't had a chance to say goodbye to Patrick, you know, Emily,' she said almost apologetically. 'I haven't seen him alone once since the storm hit.'

'Katie,' said Sarah brightly, 'this isn't the end for us—no one has given up! This is just some silly rule. Guy told me so!'

Astonishingly, Katie's voice held no fear. 'I don't see any point in fooling ourselves, Sarah. A person has a responsibility to face something like this squarely. I only wish I could have had one moment with my husband. But I won't, you know . . . he'll do his duty to the last second. That's just the way he's made.'

'Maybe we can't always say our final goodbyes, my dear,' said Emily. 'But I believe with all my heart that where there's love between a man and a woman, it's not really necessary. Patrick knows your heart and thoughts are with him now, just as

ohn knows mine are with him. The words don't
ave to be spoken aloud.'

Katie looked gratefully at Emily, one small tear
liding unheeded down her cheek. How lucky
hese women were, thought Sarah. Even now,
aced with the possibility of their deaths, they
ound a transcending strength in the bonds of love
hey shared with their husbands.

She and Guy had spoken no words either. At
east, none of the right ones. For too long her
tubborn pride had kept her from admitting the
ruth. It was Guy who had commanded her respect
nd admiration; Guy to whom she had been in-
tinctively drawn. And it was Guy whom she loved.

I love him, she thought, astonished. Yes . . . I
ove him, I love him. She said it over and over to
erself, at once intrigued and enchanted by the
ightness and simple beauty of it.

The door slid open and a group of men, bulky
n oilskins and lifejackets, crowded the deck.
Sarah's heart rose squarely to her throat as she
icked out his profile.

'Patrick,' said Captain Price, 'you and your men
o everything within your power to help Guy.'
Then, turning to Guy and laying a hand on his
houlder, he said simply, 'Good luck, son.'

'I can't believe it,' breathed Katie. 'He's
ctually going out there to try to make that
epair!'

They surged forward to the sleet-glazed rail as
he men clambered down the stairs to the main

deck. Under lines festooned with swords of ic
Guy shrugged off his life-vest and bent to receiv
the thick safety harness the men heaved over h
shoulders.

The reality of the sacrifice he was preparing
make in order to ransom their lives broke ov
Sarah with equal measures of pride and disma
She studied his face through misting eye
Already it was glazed with sharp crystals of ic
His brows and lashes were white and bristling.

His body was about to endure an appallir
ordeal. A body she had once, for a brief momen
held so close to her own . . . and then rejected.
only she could hold him to her once again ar
comfort him with her own warmth! The rush
longing for him that swept through her left h
weakened.

'Sarah?' Katie tugged at her sleeve. 'He'll mal
it—you'll see.'

'Oh, Katie,' said Sarah miserably, 'it's all wror
between us, and now I'll never be able to make
right!'

'Do . . . do you care for him, Sarah?' Kat
asked gently.

Sarah nodded, blinking back the tears.

'Look! He's going.'

Guy climbed the few steps to the catwalk th
ran out to the bow over the tangle of pipes th
littered the deck. Patrick made one last check
the tool pack strapped to his back, then gave hi
two smart slaps on his bottom. Guy turned ar

raised his hand in a gesture of farewell, and for a second, Sarah was sure his eyes looked up and fixed on hers.

She stretched out her hand as if she might touch him, and opened her mouth to call out his name, to tell him, but the wind stole her words. Devastated, she watched him turn his back to her.

The *Enterprise* groaned and heaved herself clear of the sea. Guy, the line and clamp of his harness gripped in one hand, sprinted down the long steel path. As the next wave hit, he slammed the clamp on to a metal safety bar that ran the length of the catwalk. Wedging himself between two large pipes, he held on with all the strength of his legs and arms.

A wall of glittering green water descended on him, hiding him from their eyes for agonising seconds. It finally swirled away, threatening to snap the cable that now looked so pathetically thin and suck him with it.

Again and again he performed the same desperate ritual: fighting forward a few feet, crouching, being pounded and spun around by the sucking, receding wave. It was bone-crushing, exhausting work. They watched his painful progress in silence. Thoughts for their own wellbeing were forgotten as they followed the life-and-death drama of a single man.

When he reached the forward storage tank, he dropped down from the catwalk to the deck and

snapped the harness on to a length of pipe beside
the damaged valve cover. He had at least partial
shelter there from the brunt of the waves. He
pulled the tool pack from his back and set to work
at once. He was forced to labour slowly and
clumsily in insulated gloves, since the frozen
metal would have torn the flesh from bare fingers.

He was only a small dot of colour that far away.
His progress was followed through binoculars
passed from hand to hand down the rail. After
long, dragging minutes, the man who held the
glasses trained on his distant, toy-like figure gave
a shout. Guy was waving his arms in a slow arc,
giving them the signal that he had secured the
damaged cover. A roar went up from the crowd.

'He's done it—by God, the man's done it!'
someone cried. 'We'll get out of this yet!' And for
the first time in many hours, they allowed them-
selves to hope.

But for Guy there was still the long, deadly run
back to safety. He had to make it. After he had
saved them, fate would be too cruel if it tore him
away from them now. Silence fell on them again
as he began to retrace his steps.

He was within one final sprint to the end, close
enough for them to see the agony etched across
his face. He was drawing on the very last of his
reserves. The sinews of his neck stood out in
sharp relief. His teeth were exposed in a clenched,
hard line. As another dark wall of water rose

above him, he lowered his head like a bull, his legs pumping furiously.

This time his luck did not hold. He managed to snap his harness to the bar, but as the water crashed over him, he could not find a hiding place. The pulling force of the retreating wave lifted him off his feet. The safety line pulled tight. Then, as a horrified gasp rose from the crew, it snapped with a noise like the crack of a pistol.

Sarah let out a long, agonised scream, sure she would see him swept overboard. Like a rag doll, he was tossed against a stand of pipes. As the *Enterprise* rose once more above the water, he was left hanging from the pipes, limp and seemingly without life. In the tiny whirlpools swirling beneath his dangling feet, a pool of blood grew large and tinted the water pink.

Patrick and his men made a desperate dash for him. There would be no second chances, they knew. The next wave would certainly pull him overboard. In the lull before it hit, they cut his swinging form free and dragged him in to safety.

Sarah stood in the doorway to the infirmary. They did not even see her, so fierce was their concentration. They knew his temperature had fallen close to the point where life can no longer be sustained. Warming him would have to come first, before they dealt with the head wound that had drained him of blood and consciousness.

His boots were yanked from him, releasing rivers of icy water. Scissors laid bare his arms and

legs. Someone tore away his sweater front, expos‐
ing the tangled mat of curling dark hair. The skin
that Sarah remembered as so hot and smooth was
now frighteningly blue and shrivelled.

Her eyes followed the line of his narrow hip to
where it swelled into the powerful muscle of his
thigh. How very beautiful he was, she thought,
grief constricting her throat.

A blanket snapped down over his body and four
pairs of hands began kneading, urging life back into
him. Silently, Sarah slipped out into the corridor.

By mid-morning, the storm had abated. As
Patrick predicted, the sea was glassy smooth. Life
aboard the *Enterprise* resumed its peaceful, grace‐
ful rhythm. People gathered in little knots to dis‐
cuss their adventure and Guy's heroism, but an
outsider would have seen nothing to indicate that
anything out of the ordinary had happened.

Their elation over their own survival was
tempered by the knowledge that Guy had not
regained consciousness. As soon as the ship was
within range of the coast, Sarah watched the
Enterprise's Safety Officer leave as he had come.
But this time, the helicopter was a Canadian
Armed Services' rescue vehicle, and this time
the passenger was strapped to a stretcher. There
was no flashing, hostile glance from him. Sarah
gazed down on to eyes that were closed and
sunken.

He didn't even bother to knock. Sarah looked up

from her packing to see Tony barging into her cabin.

'I want to talk to you.'

'Well, I don't want to talk to you.' She slammed the lid of her suitcase shut.

'I have to know what you're going to write about this trip.'

'Do you now?' she replied, retrieving her coat from the closet.

'You know damn well I do!'

'Look, Tony, don't you have to go and give a speech or something? I hear there's a huge welcoming committee waiting for you down on the dock.'

'Yes, there is—and I want to make sure you're not going to do something stupid to ruin things.'

Sarah pulled on her kid gloves, meticulously smoothing one finger after another, taking grim satisfaction in the way it made Tony's temper rise. 'What are you worried about? For you, it's been strictly mission accomplished. For all the outside world knows, the only real problem we had was a freak winter storm, and no one's going to blame you for that.'

'Don't toy with me, Sarah. I want to know what's going to be in that damn column of yours!'

'Then you're going to have to wait, like everybody else,' she said, clicking her bag shut. 'If you're still here when the man comes for my luggage, tell him I've gone down to my taxi already, would you?'

She closed the door on him and walked quickly down the long, polished hall, her heels making smart, brisk clicks.

All well and good to tell him to wait, she thought, as she emerged into the bright light of the Halifax morning. But the truth was, even *she* didn't have the faintest idea any longer of what she was going to write about the maiden voyage of the *Arctic Enterprise*.

CHAPTER NINE

WHEN the time did come for Sarah to write the story of the *Enterprise*, it eluded her for days. For a while, she sank into the closest thing to a real depression she had ever experienced.

She wrote a dozen different openings and tore them up in despair. She questioned her abilities, her values, and her responsibilities as a journalist. Oddly, D'Arcy had withdrawn from her during this period of testing, refusing all but the most general support. It had been, she realised only much later, his way of forcing her to come fully of age as a first-rate journalist.

Part of her problem was that so much of what happened during the height of the crisis had taken on the unreal quality of a nightmare. She was dealing with fears that did not materialise, facts that were frustratingly elusive, charges and counter-charges that could not be backed up. As Tony had warned her, there was precious little that she could set forth confidently as hard data.

Finally, with the deadline bearing down on her, she had paid a brief visit to the newspaper's legal office. Afterwards she had gone home, closed her bedroom door, and written solidly for a week.

Curiously, once the decision had been made,

the story had seemed to write itself, using her only as a vehicle. It had been there all along, waiting for her, needing only courage to uncover it.

She had wanted to tell a story about challenge and temptation, about courage and sacrifice. She wanted to describe the pressures forced on people by a world demanding fast solutions to problems to which there are no easy answers. And so she had. She analysed the questions unblinkingly, careful not to cast blame she could not prove, but refusing, also, to gloss over the very real difficulties.

Most important of all, she told a story about people—the strong, hard-working men—and women—who deal every day, often putting their lives on the line, with situations that the rest of the world only talks about.

The day she delivered the story to her editor, and sat idly chatting with Trish as she waited for him to read it, a calm had flowed into her. She was unexpectedly at peace with herself. Whatever his judgment, whether he loved it or hated it, she had written the truth as she had seen it.

From across the press room, D'Arcy's eye had caught hers and told her everything. She could have cried. After all the effort, all the private pain and misunderstanding that would never be written about, she at least had the satisfaction of knowing she had not betrayed his trust.

Trish read it, too. 'It's exciting the way you describe the storm. I shiver just reading about it.

And isn't it a miracle the way that feller managed to survive . . . what was his name?' There was curiosity in her voice.

'Court,' said Sarah. 'Guy Court.'

'Yes . . . did you ever manage to get through to the hospital in Montreal where they flew him?'

'Yes, I did,' she confirmed, her voice as matter-of-fact as she could manage. 'The nurse said it was just a mild concussion. He was able to fly back to London after only a day of rest.'

'Thank heavens for that! I wonder what his reaction to your story would be—he's such a large part of it.'

Sarah's lower lip formed a soft pout. 'It doesn't matter much. Captain Court had his mind made up about what I would write long before I did.'

Trish looked at her quizzically. The sharpness in Sarah's voice seemed quite uncalled-for. 'The phone's been ringing all morning with con-gratulations for you—I unplugged your extension, by the way,' she said. 'And D'Arcy called. He says the competition's green with envy over your scoop. He asked me to remind you about the little celebration dinner date the two of you have tonight.'

'Thanks. I won't forget. Did he say what time?'

'Eight o'clock, at the Château Laurier.'

'My, he *is* in a good mood! He's never taken me any place grander than the office cafeteria.' Sarah stirred her tea round and round. There was

nothing she could do except think of Guy. All she
was really hoping for was a chance to forget, for a
while, that small but persistent ache that had been
with her ever since she watched the helicopter
bearing Guy's body crab up and away from the
ship. She had at least to try, or the memory of
him would threaten any relationship she tried to
form with another man. No matter how deeply he
had touched her, she couldn't allow that to
happen. She was quite sure that if and when Guy
Court thought of her, he didn't let it stop him
getting on with *his* life.

Guy! she thought. Guy! He was moved to fan
whatever it was that burned in her. He drew her
out, provoked her, as she did him. It had been an
explosive love, but worth the world.

Except now she was left with ashes, and a grief
that bowed her like some great, despairing weight.
Her days were filled with regrets for a love lost.
Her nights were spent dreaming impossible
dreams. I'm frightened, she thought, suddenly. I
have all these feelings, and I don't know how to
cope with them. What am I going to do?

CHAPTER TEN

'I'M joining Mr Turner for dinner, Karl.'

The maître d'hotel was instantly attentive. Sarah was familiar to him as a newspaper personality who came with the famous to his restaurant.

'Yes, he left word, Miss Grey,' he said, smiling. 'If you'll follow me, they're already waiting.'

They? Sarah thought. She threaded her way through the crowded dining room, her dress making soft swishing noises. To lift her spirits, she had put on her best, a slip of cream silk crêpe, exquisitely tucked and edged in lace, and closed with tiny silk-covered buttons. Around her neck she wore a long strand of pearls that matched the clips on her ears.

She spotted D'Arcy sitting at a circular table by the tall windows, involved in a laughing, animated conversation with a man who sat with his back to her.

'Here's our girl at last!' said D'Arcy, beaming. He rose, as did the other man, and for a moment Sarah felt giddy and had to fight an urge to turn and flee. It was Guy.

'I'm sure no introductions are necessary between you two!' D'Arcy was saying.

'Hello, Sarah.'

She struggled for her voice. 'Hello . . . I'm glad to see you well.'

'Thank you . . . yes, I'm fine, now,' he replied, a faint, polite smile lifting the corners of his mouth.

She saw him offer his hand, saw her own accept it, becoming instantly lost in its smooth, firm grip. She prayed he would not feel the trembling that had begun to seize her.

D'Arcy held her chair for her, and mechanically she sat, aware of a quickened heartbeat.

'I tried to get in touch with you earlier to tell you about Guy's arrival in Ottawa, but we couldn't find you.' He looked down at her glass. 'We're a bit ahead of you on drinks, my dear,' he went on. 'What can I order for you?'

'A Martini, please,' she answered, startling herself, since she wasn't particularly fond of drinking. With a tremendous effort she forced her eyes to meet Guy's. 'You're here on business, I suppose, Guy,' she said.

He took a sip of his Scotch and put the glass down. 'That's right,' he replied. His voice was crisp and somewhat cold, she thought. 'I'm making rescheduling arrangements for the *Enterprise*. She didn't go back to the Arctic for a second run as we'd planned. We took her instead to Rotterdam.'

'Rotterdam . . . but why?'

'There was storm damage to repair, of course.

But the shipyard is also making some other modifications to her. Let's hope the next voyage won't be quite so hair-raising as the first.'

'I can't deny that's reassuring,' said Sarah with an attempt at lightness.

'Actually, it's a fairly major overhaul we're doing. We've managed to trace certain problems with her back to their source. In a way, I suppose, we should be grateful that we hit the worst conceivable weather on her first run.'

Sarah shuddered. 'Grateful—how can you, of all people, say that? After ... after what almost happened to you!' For the first time she allowed her eyes to rest on his face. High on his temple, almost hidden by a shock of hair, she could see the bruise, still livid and swollen, that was the result of his head being flung against the pipes.

'It put the spotlight on weaknesses, potential problems. We're not running in the dark any more, and that's what counts.'

'That will mean quite a delay in the shipment of the L.N.G., won't it?'

'It will,' he confirmed. 'Freeland will be absorbing the expense of that wait. It means the *Enterprise* will be running without profit for some time, but that's an acceptable penalty for the future benefits that will accrue to us.'

'This, by the way,' interjected D'Arcy, 'is your next assignment, Sarah—a follow-up on improvements and alterations that came as a result of the first trip. Just something small—a few paragraphs in your regular column should do it.'

Sarah's eyes were enormous and pleading. Even a few words with Guy were taxing her resources to their limit. But dear D'Arcy couldn't know that—he thought everything was falling into place beautifully. She saw the puzzlement in his eyes at her stumbled response.

'Guy has already given so much of his time for the first story, D'Arcy. I'd hate to ask him for more during an important business trip, just for a little blurb in my column.'

D'Arcy frowned. 'But he's already offered, Sarah. And I don't think I twisted his arm too hard . . . did I, Guy?'

'Of course not,' Guy replied smoothly. 'I'm sure Sarah and I can arrange an hour or so that's mutually convenient.' The absolute calm of the man only underscored her own jangled nerves. 'I feel I owe you that much for the story you did on us,' he said, looking back at her.

'You've seen it, then?' she asked, flushing. She had completely forgotten the morning paper.

'Yes. And on behalf of Freeland Shipping, I'd like to thank you for it, Sarah.'

'That's not necessary,' she said stiffly, conscious of the impersonal tone he was using. 'Besides,' she added, this time more softly, 'I'm sure I needn't point out to you that the article wasn't entirely positive—I'm sorry about that . . . truly.'

'There were criticisms, to be sure. But they

ere fair, and they were well balanced. A sensa-
onalist, someone less ethical, could have devas-
ated us.'

This time she spoke without hesitation. 'Those
eople didn't deserve to be dragged through the
ud, Guy. I don't know when I've ever met a
roup of people who impressed me more than the
rew of that ship. They were wonderful, and I
elt they deserved to have their story told.'

She broke off suddenly, uncomfortably aware
f the strange way he was looking at her. It was as
the ghost of his cousin was sitting there with
em. Was Guy still trying to understand where
ony fitted into all this? She retreated into silence
s the waiter brought their food.

The meal passed in agony for her. The usually
oised and self-contained woman, at ease in the
ost exalted company, found herself fumbling for
ords, awkward with her food, afraid, even, of
pilling her wine.

A few weeks before she had stood on the decks
f the *Enterprise* and ached for the chance to tell
his man that she loved him. Now, observing his
etached, reserved demeanour, she felt chilled
nd knew that it could never happen.

The men had just been served their brandy
hen she gathered up her bag and gloves. 'Sarah,
ou're not leaving us already!' chided D'Arcy.

'I'm sorry,' she said breathlessly. 'I've got to
e up very early tomorrow ... I promised
omeone I'd go skiing.'

'But you haven't even set up an appointme
with Guy yet,' he reminded her, this time wi
real irritation in his voice.

'I'll . . . I'll call you tomorrow morning, Gu
she said.

'You won't be here,' he pointed out.

'Then Monday. Where are you staying—he
at the Château?'

To her dismay he was at her side, draping h
fur jacket over her shoulders. 'Since Sarah fin
herself so pressed for time, D'Arcy, perhaps you
excuse the both of us. I can take Sarah home a
we can discuss it on the way.'

'That's really not necessary, Guy . . . I have n
own car outside anyway.'

'Then I'll drive you and take a taxi back,' I
said, unperturbed.

She began to protest again, but felt his har
close tightly and meaningly over her elbow. Aft
thanking his host, he propelled her firmly throug
the maze of tables as if she were something I
owned. In front of all those watchful eyes she d
not dare protest. Once in the lobby, though, sl
pulled her arm from his grasp and said brisk
'Can't we just set up a time now, Guy? This real
isn't necessary!'

'I know that. But I'm going with you anyway
he announced curtly. 'Stay here while I get n
coat.'

She fumed silently at the familiar dictatori
manner. But she waited.

Later, slipping into the seat beside her, he put out his hand wordlessly for the keys. With an impatient flick she dropped them into his palm.

'Are you really going skiing tomorrow?' he asked, looking back over his shoulder as he eased them out of their slot.

'No,' she said with defiant bluntness. 'I lied.'

'I thought so. That was rather rude,' he said reproachfully.

She ignored that. 'You have to make a left turn here to get to my place,' she said flatly.

'I know where you live. But I want to drive for while. I enjoy it. You don't mind, do you?'

Sarah sighed and looked out the window at the blurring lines of car lights in the frosty night. Guy drove as she thought he would, quickly and with careless ease. They were quiet for a while, and she found herself untensing just a little, enjoying it as he did.

'Tony's out of Freelands,' he said at last, shattering the stillness. His voice was quiet but almost brutal.

So a final confrontation over Tony was not to be avoided after all, she thought with a kind of sad resignation. She supposed it had to be, and it might provide the only satisfaction of their ill-fated relationship. But what had he meant by 'out'?

'I don't understand,' she said, turning to face him. 'How can Tony be out of his own company?'

He stared straight ahead. Passing cars shot their lights into the car. In the moving beams she caught the tic of a jaw muscle, the compression of his lips. 'He's sold his stock in the company to Uncle Julian and me. He has absolutely no position in Freeland Shipping any longer.'

Sarah tilted her head to one side and tried to understand what he was telling her. 'Just like that?'

'Just like that. He made no conditions on the transfer of either the stock or the power, and the lawyers tied the whole thing up very quickly.'

'But shipping is Tony's passion, Guy, his obsession in life! I heard him threaten to force *you* out of the company.'

He gave her a quick, sardonic glance. 'Did you really think he could survive as director after what happened up there?'

Sarah spread her hands in a gesture of confusion. 'But what *did* happen up there—a violent storm, some equipment breakdown because of it? The bottom line is still that the trip was a success. I may suspect otherwise, and you no doubt *know* otherwise—but to the rest of the world, the only culprit was that freak storm.'

Guy swung the car into a parking space overlooking the frozen canal where a few hardy skaters were still tracing figures under the stars. He cut the motor and for a moment she thought she could hear the pounding of her heart.

'How much of that . . . argument did you overhear, Sarah?'

'The important part, I suppose,' she replied
quietly. 'I heard you accuse Tony of altering your
design specifications and using substandard
materials in the construction.'

He nodded. 'Tony was very clever. He was right
in predicting that I could never prove any wilful
wrongdoing on his part. Everything he did was
within the letter, if not the spirit, of the law. But
he slipped up here and there. One big mistake he
made was in underestimating Uncle Julian. Even
at the low point of his illness, he still kept a finger on the pulse of the company. He was far too
sharp, too experienced, not to realise Tony was
pulling off the *Enterprise* too fast and in-
expensively.'

'You suspected nothing?' she probed gently.

'No. Guy the Great missed it. Did you think
such a thing was possible?' There was just a touch
of amusement in his voice. 'Once I finished with
the design phase, I pulled out because of my other
obligations. Tony was left on his own to oversee
the construction. He was right, you know, Sarah,'
he said. 'If I hadn't been off playing hero, I'd
have seen what was going on right under my nose.
You can charge a lot of the blame for what
happened up to Guy the Great. Does that give
you satisfaction?'

'But you came!' she cried. 'In the end, when
you were needed, you were there.'

'I wouldn't have been, Sarah, if it weren't for
my uncle. He had nothing specific to go on, only

his intuition that something was awry. It was
who ordered me back from South Africa in ti[m]
to catch the *Enterprise* before she reached t[he]
Arctic.'

Sarah gave a small shudder of horror and d[is]taste. 'When I think that Tony could actually [do]
something like that! To play with people's lives [to]
further his own ambitions! And why would he ri[sk]
having a reporter on board if there was a pos[si]bility of things going wrong?' she said, her voi[ce]
lifting in wonder. 'It was a terrific gamble!'

'Tony's not the monster you may think him [to]
be, Sarah,' he answered quietly.

'There can't be an excuse!' she retort[ed]
sharply.

'No, not an excuse. But if you knew Tony a[s I]
do, you'd at least see how he could fall into suc[h a]
trap. He's always coasted through life on his po[si]tion. He was hopelessly indulged by his paren[ts.]
He never developed the discipline to study, n[or]
the patience to wait for others to do it for hi[m.]
He put a lot of blind trust into technology [he]
didn't understand. He never came to grips wi[th]
the implications of what he had done in allowi[ng]
subtle alterations in the *Enterprise*'s design. B[ut]
when he finally did, he was appalled.'

'I don't understand you, Guy,' she insiste[d,]
shaking her head. 'You're defending him, after [all]
he did!'

'No,' he said firmly, 'I'm not defending hi[m.]
But he's my cousin, and I have to at least try [to]

athom him. He was frightened, Sarah . . . he was
truly frightened by what happened that day. He
wants no part of shouldering that sort of re-
ponsibilty ever again. He was only too happy to
bow out.'

Sarah's thick lashes swept her cheeks. 'You
almost died,' she said softly, unable to find it in
her own heart to forgive Tony.

He took her tiny, gloved hand and studied it
intently, turning it over in his two hands and
running a finger lightly down her palm. She held
her breath and didn't dare pull away.

He raised his eyes to meet hers. 'I've read your
story a dozen times today—it's terrific. I don't
know how you managed to extract it so beautifully
from such an overwhelming experience. It's all
here, everything that's important. Sarah . . . I
know that you never played an active role in
Tony's plans.'

She turned her face away from him quickly,
clinging to just a little pride. 'But you thought I
did, once,' she said raggedly. 'You assumed that I
was grasping, or gullible enough, to be manipu-
ated by him.'

'Yes . . . and no,' he said, refusing to release
her hand. 'As soon as I saw you I knew what
Tony was up to. He wanted publicity very badly,
publicity of a very personal, self-glorifying kind.
Your closeness to him, your acceptance of his
invitation to Fairfield . . . and your hostility to
me—it all seemed to reinforce the conclusion

that I'd jumped to.'

'*My* hostility to you!' she cried, real anguish
her voice. 'How else could I have reacted, give
the way you attacked me at every turn!'

Guy nodded his agreement at once. 'I know,
know. I behaved very badly towards you. I wa
so damn conflicted! My head told me one thir
about you, but my instincts told me somethir
quite different. I knew you were too intelligen
too spirited to be a part of it, and yet—oh, Sara!
the only defence I can offer for my behaviour
that I was half out of my mind wondering if w
were all sailing for disaster and I didn't know ho
to begin to save us. Forgive me—please.'

He was silent, waiting, and she knew what sh
had to do. Now that she knew the whole story
she could see what a terrifying burden he ha
been carrying, alone. For a man of Guy's tem
perament, such a naked apology could not hav
come cheaply.

'Of course I forgive you, Guy—if forgiveness
really necessary. I . . . I'm ashamed myself if
made your task any more difficult than it alread
was.' She spoke slowly, choosing her words care
fully, finding it agony to control the emotion tha
was bubbling up inside her. 'This whole situatio
between us has been . . . difficult for me. It's
relief to have it settled, to feel that all the loos
ends have been tied up at last.'

'Are they? Really? I don't think so . . . don't w
have one conversation to finish?'

'What conversation?' she asked.

'Just before I went out to the bow to secure that cover, I looked back. You said something to me.'

'You heard me?' she said, suddenly and inexplicably afraid. Two red patches appeared on her cheeks.

'No, I didn't. But I'd like to, now. Sarah,' he said, with strained patience, 'if I can fly across the ocean just to say "I beg your pardon", surely you can do me the courtesy of repeating what you said to me that morning.'

'You didn't fly here for that,' she replied reprovingly.

'There was nothing I did here today that couldn't have been handled just as well by telephone. And I didn't just happen into your editor's office this afternoon to thank him for the story. Now, are you going to answer me?'

She looked at him and in the pale glow of the street light saw the smile that played about those precious lines beside his eyes. Suddenly her fear drained away and she felt suffused by a calm acceptance of whatever was to be. Her eyes returned his gaze, clear and unarmoured.

'I said . . . be careful . . . and I love you.'

'That's what I thought, or prayed,' he said tenderly. He laid his fingers softly on her flushed cheek. 'Sarah darling—I love you too. Couldn't you tell—wasn't it written all over me!'

'Love . . . no, no, just so much anger, Guy!'

'I was angry, dearest. And frustrated. I couldn't

seem to get through to you. And I couldn't stand the thought of you being with Tony. That's why I took you on that sightseeing trip. I wanted to get you away from his influence, if only for a few hours.'

'And when you made love to me that night—or tried to—it wasn't just . . .'

Guy took her face between his two large hands. His voice roughened. 'It was because I loved you with all my heart, Sarah.'

She laughed then, very, very gently. The surge of joy in her was so sweet. So much pain, so much confusion and misunderstanding was behind them. But when his lips found hers there was only silence for long, infinitely beautiful minutes.

'Marry me, Sarah Grey,' he whispered at last, his voice low and urgent. 'It won't be quiet and it won't be uneventful, but I promise you a life worth living to the fullest!'

No, she thought. It won't be a particularly peaceful marriage. There will be times of loneliness and separation. Even fear. But it would be all the more precious for it. No other man could offer her this.

'Yes,' she whispered, 'yes,' and again there was the silence, broken only by soft and loving sighs.

It was only the chill that began to permeate the car that forced Guy to tear himself away from her and the exquisitely pleasurable pain they gave each other.

'I want to marry you as soon as we can get the

licence,' he said. 'I want to take you back with
me next week, Sarah.'

'I believe you're serious!' she said.

'Perhaps it's the work I do,' he explained, 'but
I've come to believe you have to seize your
chances in life, Sarah. Live it when you can, as
well as you can. I want you with me, darling, and
I don't see any reason for putting it off one second
longer than we must.'

'You make me dizzy, Guy—but I love it. Don't
ever stop!'

'I have only one regret, Sarah, and that's your
job. When I read your story and talked to D'Arcy
about you, I knew just how gifted you are and
how hard you've worked to be where you are. I
don't have any right to ask you to give that up,
and yet it seems as if circumstances are making
me do just that.'

A wisp of cloud floated before Sarah's sun. It
dimmed the light in her heart for only the briefest
moment. 'I like to grab hold of my chances in
life, too, darling,' she said. 'I have a very portable
talent. We'll be travelling a lot, I assume. I'll be
having experiences I couldn't have hoped for
without you. I'll freelance!'

He drove with one hand, holding her fingers to
his lips. 'You're wonderful,' he said, laughing.

'No,' she said firmly, 'just inspired by you.
What woman wouldn't be?'

'Financially,' he said, his tone more serious,
'we'll be a little bit tighter than I had thought. I

didn't want to get into it with your boss there, but it took just about everything I own to buy out Tony. On top of that, Uncle Julian and I had to cover the losses on the *Enterprise* out of personal funds. In fact, my uncle is disposing of his London house to generate some cash.'

'But what will he do, Guy?'

'He's moving permanently to Fairfield to live with my mother. It's not much of a hardship, really. He's been looking forward to retiring there with his gardens and dogs for some time now. If you can stand living in the middle of a hurricane, I thought we'd make it our home base for a while, too. There's a gatehouse on the property we can fix up any way that pleases you. It won't be for long, darling. Just another year or so until the *Enterprise*'s paying her way again. Until then, I'm afraid I'm wealthy only on paper. But I promise you we'll have a place in the city and a country house of our own as soon as I sort out this mess Tony's put us in!'

'Guy, I don't care about the money!'

'I know. But I do—for your sake. I want to assure you the kind of life you deserve. And I will.'

'I don't doubt that for a moment, although just being with you like this seems heaven enough.'

'Do you realise,' he said sternly, 'that I've never seen you when you haven't been bundled and swathed right up to your adorable nose in sweaters and furs and scarves?'

Sarah felt a pleasant flush. 'Winter can't last for ever, darling.'

'I know, but I'm impatient. You must be remarkable in a bikini. I've been asked to look over an oil tanker that's docked right now in Indonesia. It's lush and tropical there, Sarah . . . and·warm. How does that sound as a honeymoon destination?'

So, she thought, it's starting already. A life full of the new and unexpected. How does that make me feel? she wondered. Excited? Yes, but less so than she might have expected. Frightened? No, not a bit. She felt at peace, she thought, astonished, as if some hunger deep inside her had at last been satisfied. She made a small murmur of contentment. Smiling, Guy draped his arm over her shoulders and hugged her.

'Indonesia sounds just fine,' she said, and burrowed deeper into his warmth.

Harlequin Plus

A WORD ABOUT THE AUTHOR

Linda Harrel has always been busy with people. In Chicago she was involved with a children's aid society. In New York she worked at a day-care center for abused children. And in Toronto, where she now makes her home with her husband and son, she was a social worker.

It was while in this last position that Linda was introduced to Harlequin. Seeing the pleasure that a Harlequin novel gave to one of her cases, a young welfare mother, she decided to read the book herself. She found it to be a beautifully written novel—and it touched her.

So much so, it seems, that she was moved to write her own Harlequin. When the manuscript was completed, she submitted it for publication; though it was rejected, her second try, *Sea Lightning* (Romance #2337), was accepted. Linda was hooked. There was nothing more she wanted to do than continue writing.

Linda Harrel is still busy with people—but now they are characters in her delightful books.

Sample a first taste of the #RED... Subscribe and subscription description on the following page